# After the Wallpaper Music

## Jean Mills

pajamapress

**First published in Canada and the United States in 2024**

Text copyright © 2024 Jean Mills
This edition copyright © 2024 Pajama Press Inc.
This is a first edition.

10 9 8 7 6 5 4 3 2 1

All rights reserved. No part of this publication may be reproduced, stored in a retrieval system or transmitted, in any form or by any means, without the prior written consent of the publisher or a licence from The Canadian Copyright Licensing Agency (Access Copyright). For an Access Copyright licence, visit www.accesscopyright.ca or call toll free 1.800.893.5777.

www.pajamapress.ca                info@pajamapress.ca

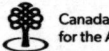  

The publisher gratefully acknowledges the support of the Canada Council for the Arts and the Ontario Arts Council for its publishing program. We acknowledge the financial support of the Government of Canada through the Canada Book Fund (CBF) for our publishing activities.

**Library and Archives Canada Cataloguing in Publication**

Title: After the wallpaper music / Jean Mills.
Names: Mills, Jean, 1955- author.
Identifiers: Canadiana 20240358171 | ISBN 9781772783223 (hardcover)
Subjects: LCGFT: Novels.
Classification: LCC PS8576.I5654 A79 2024 | DDC jC813/.54—dc23

**Cataloging-in-Publication Data (U.S.)**

Names: Mills, Jean, 1955-, author.

Title: After the wallpaper music / Jean Mills.

Description: First edition. | Toronto, Ontario : Pajama Press, 2024. | Summary: "Flora wants her string quartet to play a classical song for the Battle of the Bands competition, while her friends want to play something new. But when Simon, a talented drummer who is struggling with a recent loss, invites Flora to join his rock trio, she discovers that finding harmony with her friends, music, and family just became more complicated"--Provided by publisher.

Identifiers: ISBN 978-1-77278-322-3 (hardcover)

Subjects: LCSH: Musicians – Juvenile fiction. | Music -- Competitions – Juvenile fiction. | Grief – Juvenile fiction. | Friendship – Juvenile fiction. | BISAC: JUVENILE FICTION / Performing Arts / Music. | JUVENILE FICTION / Social Themes / Friendship. | JUVENILE FICTION / Social Themes / Death, Grief, Bereavement. | JUVENILE FICTION / School & Education. | JUVENILE FICTION / Family / Multigenerational.

Classification: LCC PZ7. M657 AF258 2024 | DDC [Fic] – dc23

Cover art by Scot Ritchie
Cover and book design by Simin Dewji

This book was designed with left alignment and generous spacing to improve the reading experience for readers of all neurotypes.

Manufactured in China

**Pajama Press Inc.**
11 Davies Avenue, Suite 103, Toronto, Ontario Canada, M4M 2A9

Distributed in Canada by UTP Distribution
5201 Dufferin Street Toronto, Ontario Canada, M3H 5T8

Distributed in the U.S. by Publishers Group West
1 Ingram Blvd. La Vergne, TN 37086, USA

For Charlie and Jack.
I hope you'll play me
some tunes someday...

—J.M.

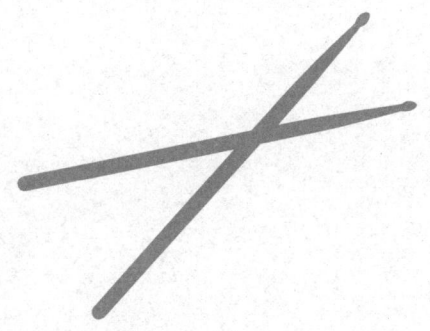

For Charlie and dad,
I hope you'll play me
some tunes someday.

J. M.

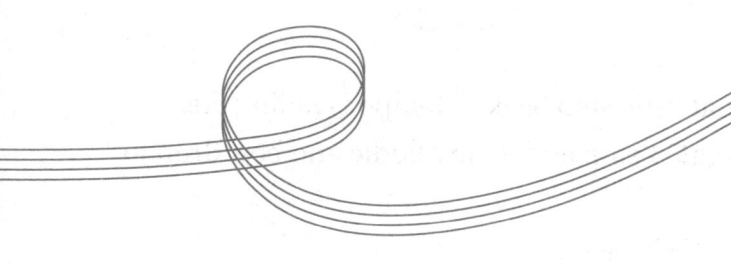

# 𝄞 Chapter 1

"SLOWER," SAYS AUNTIE FLORA.

She means business. I know this because she's tapping her walking stick (she won't let us call it a "cane") on the floor and it's one tiny, syncopated split-second off the tempo I'm using for "The Super Jig Set." There's no messing around with Auntie Flora when she has her mind made up about something.

This is her superpower—getting people to do what she wants.

Of course, I play slower. Drag the bow just a little bit more over the strings. It's hard, though. Auntie Flora knows her jigs and reels, for sure. But my fiddle and I feel that "The Super Jig Set" is totally about rocking out.

Taking that little step back in tempo is killing me.

"Aaargh!" I stop and let my fiddle and bow drop to my sides.

"What?" she asks.

"It's HARD!" I say, frowning at her. "Playing it slower is hard."

"It's not hard," she lifts her chin at me. "It's a tune, not a race. Not a get-it-done-before-the-kettle-boils kind of thing. Play it right. Come on, Flora. Try it again."

Yes, I'm Flora too. Named for her. It's true.

As Great Aunts go, though, I could do worse. Auntie Flora has been living in the basement suite of our house since she had a fall last winter while shoveling snow on the sidewalk of her own little house three towns away. My parents had said, *That's it, Auntie Flora, you're moving in with us.* And she said, *Not on your life.* And my father said, *Yes on your life, and just think, you'll get to hear Flora playing tunes day and night.* And that was it. My fiddle sealed the deal.

So, part of the deal is me playing tunes on my fiddle for her in the evening after homework. And after practicing those other kinds of tunes on my violin, which is actually also my fiddle.

To clarify, I play first violin in the Arden Youth Music Center's string quartet with my friends Kristy,

Bas, and Vlad. We all came through the music program there, and when we hit middle school, our music teacher, Mrs. García, went nuts. *A ready-made string quartet! Kids who can already play stringed instruments and know who Haydn is!* We are the Arden Middle School's official string quartet (as of Grade Six). We are booked for every school event. Parents' Meet the Teacher Night (known in our house as Meet The Creature Night) in late September. Holidays of every culture and denomination. Random "Arts Celebration" events. And even the occasional benefit concert for the Youth Music Center, or for someone's wedding (Miss Turner became Mrs. Kalandar in June and we played her down and up the aisle).

But my violin has magic powers and transforms into a fiddle at night, and that's when I play the old Newfoundland tunes for Auntie Flora. As fast as I can.

No, no, no. I don't play fast to get it over with and leave Auntie Flora to her movies ("Oh, I just watch that nonsense to pass the time," she says as she settles in for another silly romcom).

I play fast because the tunes just fall under my fingers and fly out, faster and faster. And it fills me with such a feeling that I can't even describe it.

"Slow down," orders Auntie Flora.

And you know, it kills me just a little, but I do.

"Better?" I ask her.

"Parson's Pond Jig" continues, just the tiniest bit slower.

"Perfect, Ducky," she says, and closes her eyes, smiling, and taps along.

# Chapter 2

THE NEW BOY IN OUR CLASS IS NAMED SIMON DELUCA, AND all we know about him is that his sister was killed in a car accident over the summer.

Not strictly true. We know something else about him. His father was the lead guitarist in a Garage Rock band called House Party that was big on all the rock music playlists back in the 2000s.

"This is amazing," my mother said one July morning in a voice that made me look up from the sudoku. (We have a "No screens at the breakfast table" rule. An actual, real, printed-on-paper newspaper is delivered every morning to our front door. We have an orderly distribution method for who gets what first.

Mom, front section. Dad, Business. Me, puzzles. My older sister Agnes—well, Agnes is usually still in bed at this point). Mom's mouth was an "O" and her eyebrows were sky-high.

"What's amazing?" I asked. My mother is usually the steady, smiling type who doesn't find many things *amazing*, so this was an unusual reaction for her to have while reading the paper.

"Theo DeLuca is moving here, to Arden." She looked over at Dad, who was leaning on the counter with his first cup of coffee and his eyes on his phone. (Yes, standing at the counter with a screen is okay). "It's right here, in this interview on the Arts page. *The* Theo DeLuca."

Dad looked up at her and they exchanged a look.

"House Party Theo DeLuca?" he asked. "Moving here? Whatever for? I thought he was holed up on some island out on the West Coast or something."

Mom scanned the article she was reading and nodded. "He's joining the Faculty of Music at the university. Something about a grant, and a chair. Oh!" She raised her eyebrows and leaned back. "Whole family coming. Wife Petra—remember her? Wife number three…or was it four? Wasn't she a backup singer or something?" She looked back down at the article and read out loud. "'*I guess I've got something to offer to young musicians. And maybe it's time to experience a different part of the country,*' says DeLuca with his trademark drawl. '*You know, less West Coast, more real life.*'" Mom sat back and frowned. "What the heck does that mean?"

"Wasn't there something about his daughter?" Dad asked and Mom started reading the article again.

"Right. Right, a few months ago," she said, frowning again.

I had no idea what was going on. Who was Theo DeLuca? What was House Party? What happened to the daughter?

But I was no closer to knowing because at that moment we heard the slow steps of Auntie Flora coming up from her downstairs suite and Dad put his phone down to fill up the kettle. Auntie Flora is not a coffee drinker. It's all tea with her. Tea, all day long.

"Good morning," she chirped as she entered the kitchen, gray hair pulled back in a tidy bun, cane—I meant, walking stick—in her hand.

And it all went into routine from there, with Auntie Flora settling into her chair at the table, milk and sugar and her favorite mug set down in front of her, and conversation about "How did you sleep?" and "What have you got planned today?" while the kettle boiled.

And Theo DeLuca and his move to Arden was forgotten.

But not by me.

♫

A quick internet search revealed that Theo DeLuca was lead guitarist in a Seattle-based band called House Party. Huge underground following but not mainstream. Radio stations couldn't play much of their music because of the swear words. Guitar work that set the standard. Wild lifestyle. Blah blah blah.

And then I found the personal stuff. A court appearance for some drug offence about twenty years ago. Two divorces, three marriages. Multiple children and...

*Tragic death of Theo DeLuca's daughter in vehicle accident,* said the Google entry.

I felt cold, but I clicked the link and kept reading.

Grace DeLuca. She was eight years old. Car driven by her father. Mother Petra also injured but okay. Son Simon not injured. No charges laid. Blinding rainstorm, winding mountain road, oncoming traffic...

I shut my laptop and wrapped my arms around myself.

And after that, I tried not to think about Theo, Petra, Simon, or Grace DeLuca.

And I didn't think about them again, until today, on the second day of Grade Eight at Arden Middle School, when new kid Simon DeLuca is sitting in my classroom, and no one but me seems to have any idea who he is.

Yesterday, on the first day of Grade Eight, Mr. Petrillo had told us that we would be welcoming a new classmate, which is a big deal in our little town, where we've all known each other since birth and are even, in some cases, distant cousins.

"We need to be especially aware of Simon," Mr. Petrillo had said, leaving out his last name—on purpose? Maybe. "His family has suffered a terrible loss over the summer. They were in a car accident, and Simon's young sister died."

Silence in the room, and a quick drawing in of breath from Sophie Andrews, who lost her older brother, Jackson, in a car accident two years ago. No one glanced at her, or at Tim, whose grandfather died last summer in an accident on the farm.

"Death is part of life," Auntie Flora had said softly as she sat with me after Jackson's funeral and stroked my head softly, over and over, as I cried. He was only a few years older than me. "It's not fair, so it's okay to cry. But then we go and be kind."

That didn't really help.

But I know what she meant. And I knew that's why Mr. Petrillo was telling us about Simon DeLuca.

But, we quickly realize, Simon DeLuca is a hard person to be kind to.

# Chapter 3

"WANT TO SIT WITH US FOR LUNCH?" VLAD ASKS SIMON AS we're all at our lockers.

Vlad is that guy. The friendly guy. The helpful guy. The "Do you need help cleaning the boards, Ms. Stillman?" guy.

Vlad is what Auntie Flora calls "a giver."

So it's not surprising to anyone that Vlad is the one to step up beside Simon DeLuca, the new boy.

Vlad is almost six feet tall, so he towers over Simon, who is about the same height as me (which is five feet, five inches). Though, I can't be sure, of course. I haven't stood that close to Simon, and he sits on the other side of the classroom from me.

Actually, he sits slumped with his shaggy hair hanging down over his face, so it's hard to tell much about him. Brown eyes, I think. A very straight mouth, possibly frowning.

(If I had lost my sister in a car accident and was stuck at a new school, in a new town, with a father who's known for being a drug-using rock star with a swearing issue, I might be frowning too.)

Simon pauses, looks up at Vlad and then down at his locker.

"Hi," he mumbles, still looking at his lock, concentrating on the numbers. He has long slender fingers, I notice. I wonder if he's a musician, too?

"Would you like to sit with me and my friends for lunch today? With everything so new, I thought you might like some company," Vlad smiles.

Simon opens his locker door, and tosses his books in.

"No, thanks. I'm okay," he says without looking at Vlad.

Vlad keeps smiling, but he glances at us and shrugs.

"Are you sure? I could introduce you around, if you want." Vlad is nothing if not persistent.

But Simon still has his eyes on his locker.

"No. Thanks. But no. I'd rather be alone," he says to his locker.

Kristy elbows me and we walk by, throwing a glance at Vlad, who is still looking down at Simon.

"That was just rude!" Kristy whispers to me as we reach our lockers.

I shrug. Yes, maybe.

I glance back and see Vlad nodding and saying, still friendly, "Okay," to Simon (who doesn't even seem to notice). Vlad steps away and walks across the hall to his own locker. Bas looks at him and makes a *What was that?* face. Vlad just shrugs.

Simon has closed his locker and is now walking away down the hallway, shoulders hunched and a phone up to his ear. Many eyes watch him go.

"So rude!" Kristy says again.

I watch Simon DeLuca walk down the hall ignoring the crowd around him as he disappears into it.

*Rude*. I wonder what Auntie Flora would say.

# 🎼 Chapter 4

"BUT HE JUST STOOD THERE, BASICALLY IGNORING YOU, said 'no' to lunch, and then he walked away, Vlad," Kristy says.

We four are in our usual pod, ambling along the sidewalk toward the Arden Youth Music Center after school.

"I know, but he didn't actually say anything rude," says Vlad. "He just didn't want to hang out with us, I guess."

Vlad carries his cello on his back in a special backpack kind of thing. He's so tall, it sits there quite comfortably. Thank goodness I'm not a cellist. I'd be bent over and staggering down the sidewalk.

"Well, I thought he was rude. Why wouldn't he want to hang out with us? Does he think he's better than us or something?" Kristy says, viola case bouncing off her leg. She likes carrying her instrument where everyone can see it. Yes, she's a bit of a show-off, but she's funny about it. *Violas need more love in this world,* she says. *I'm just making sure people see my gorgeous Dorothy.* Yes, her viola is named Dorothy. And yes, violas do need more love because there are so many bad viola jokes. For example, *How do you keep your violin from being stolen? Answer: put it in a viola case.*

I think Kristy's viola is gorgeous, and she plays it beautifully. So I don't mind at all when she swings her case at her side, covers it in stickers, and shows it off to draw attention.

"I don't know," says Bas. "Maybe he's just shy."

And Bas would know, being a bit on the shy side himself. His head is always bowed forward a bit. He has a soft voice, too. He doesn't like to be the center of attention, which is maybe why he's so comfortable playing second violin next to me. And when he plays, you would never call him shy. He's amazing.

"That's what I think," says Vlad, nodding. "Shy. And it must be weird to be in a new school. And there's also all that bad stuff that happened."

He means the car accident and Simon's little sister, of course. We're all quiet for a moment, thinking about that.

"I guess," Kristy says after a minute. "Okay. He gets a pass on the lunch invitation, then. But I'm watching him."

Oh dear. Poor Simon DeLuca.

Mr. Herndorff is waiting for us in the practice room when we arrive.

"Before we get started," he says over the clicking of case latches as we get our instruments out and start tuning. "I have something big to tell you."

Okay, that stops us.

"Something big?" Vlad looks around at us all. "Could be good. Could be bad."

"Oh, this is good," says Mr. Herndorff. He's practically rubbing his hands together in excitement as he settles onto the high stool he sits on during our practices. "You're going to love it."

Kristy and Vlad sit up straight, always ready for some excitement. Maybe it's a music festival invitation. Or a visiting instructor from the symphony? That's always cool. But Bas and I wait, because I've learned that *good* and *you're going to love it* can mean quite different things to adults than it does to kids.

"Battle of the Bands," Mr. Herndorff says. "The board of directors has voted to run a Battle of the Bands competition, right here at the Center. In four weeks. And I hope you're okay with it, because I've already tentatively entered you. Just need the permission forms signed by your parents."

He waves some papers at us.

"Are we considered a 'band'?" Vlad asks. "I mean, isn't a band more like guitars and drums and someone singing loudly into a mic?"

That's kind of what I was thinking. You don't usually hear of a classical music string quartet being called "a band." But Mr. Herndorff is smiling and nodding.

"You are totally a band," he says. "Anything goes in this competition. The idea is to get kids playing, singing, performing. So you guys are in, and you can play whatever you want. Doesn't have to be the Haydn."

"Anything?" Vlad's face tells me he's already thinking outside the box. "Like, the theme music from a movie or something? *Manchester*? Or maybe *Jurassic Park*?"

Mr. Herndorff tips his head to the side, thinking.

"I guess if we can source the music in string quartet format, yes." He smiles and rubs his hands together, like a kid getting excited about doing something a bit different. "Why not?"

"What's the prize?" Yes, trust Kristy to think of that.

"Well, there's a sponsor with ties to the Radio City Music Hall in New York. The winners will get tickets to a concert of their choice! Isn't that fantastic?"

The Radio City Music Hall is where Dad and Mom took Agnes and me to hear one of their favorite singers, some guy with a million records and a very '90s vibe. Agnes and I were probably the youngest people there, but, hey, live music is always awesome, so it was great.

"So, what do you say?" Mr. Herndorff looks around at us. "You in? Is this a go?"

The four of us grin at each other. A trip to New York City with a concert of our choice?

"We're in!"

"It'll be a lot of work, you realize," he says to us because, of course, that's what he has to say.

But I can't wait to get started on rehearsals, because playing my violin never feels like work to me.

I look at the rest of the band and we all grin at each other. This is going to be so fun!

At least, that's how it starts out.

# Chapter 5

"DRUMS," SAYS SIMON DELUCA. "PLEASE."

Mrs. García and Simon are standing at the front of the music room having a conversation before class starts.

"As I explained, we already have two percussion players, Simon," Mrs. García says. Actually, she repeats.

The room has gone unusually quiet as we watch this little drama unfold between our teacher and the new boy. It's the first class for our joint Strings and Band classes, and since Simon wasn't here for the first Band class earlier in the week, he missed out on choosing his preferred instrument. Awkward for Mrs. G. I bet she's wishing she was doing this somewhere other than the front of the classroom with an audience.

"The available instruments for students in the Band option are bassoon, clarinet, or trumpet," says Mrs. García, smiling at Simon and using her calm teacher voice. "I'm really sorry, but those are the only instruments available for this class."

Our heads swivel from her to Simon.

He's standing there looking at the floor. Embarrassed? No, I don't think so. More like—kind of mad? That sort of "you can't tell me what to do" look that some people get. Agnes is a pro at it.

I glance back at Rudy and Pierre, our percussion section, and they are clearly unsure how this is going to end up. They've been the percussion section—which is a drum kit, cymbals, a couple of djembes, a triangle, a cowbell, an ancient glockenspiel, a xylophone, and an egg shaker that everyone wants a turn at—since the first day of Grade Seven, although Rudy has been known to sit at the piano, too. And, no, the piano is not considered an official school music class instrument.

But Simon DeLuca wouldn't know anything about that. He's clearly fixated on percussion.

He doesn't say anything. He just looks at her, then down at the floor. Silent.

Kristy catches my eye from the viola section and makes a face that probably means, *See? Rude.*

In the long uncomfortable silence, I watch Simon, and I don't see rude. I see this boy with long hair that hides his face, hands clenching and unclenching, just because he really, really wants to play the drums and this teacher won't let him.

I wish I could do something, but what?

I turn and look over my shoulder at Rudy, who sees me and shrugs.

"Simon?" Mrs. García says. "I'm sorry you can't have your first choice, but these other options will give you an opportunity to learn and grow your music skills, I promise you. Would you like to discuss this after class? Maybe try one of the other instruments for today?"

But it's not Simon who answers. It's Rudy.

"You know, Mrs. G.," Rudy says from the back of the room. "I don't mind switching to trumpet. I mean, I've had a year on beats with Pierre here, and you know? Trumpet is pretty cool." He shrugs. "Wynton Marsalis, right?"

I see Simon DeLuca's hands twitch and loosen. He looks at Rudy sideways under that screen of long hair.

"Oh, well, that could be very helpful, Rudy." Mrs. García turns to smile at him. She looks a bit relieved.

"Louis Armstrong, too," Vlad says, turning around

in the cello section and nodding. "You could be the next Miles Davis. You even kinda look like him. The hair, you know?"

"Exactly!" Rudy nods and runs a hand through his long curly hair.

"Well, okay then, Rudy," Mrs. García nods and smiles. Oh yes, she's definitely relieved. "There you go, Simon. Drums it is. And, of course, everything else in the percussion section."

Simon looks up at her then.

"Thank you," he says.

And then he turns and walks to the back of the music room, to Rudy, and puts out his hand and they do some complicated handshake thing that only some people (athletes? musicians?) know how to do, and he says, "Thanks."

"No problem. All yours," says Rudy. "Friends don't let friends clap on one and three, right?"

Percussion humor.

"Right."

And for the first time, I see Simon DeLuca smile.

# 𝄞 Chapter 6

"ALL RIGHT," SAYS DAD, AS HE PUTS THE BREADBASKET ON the table and sits down. "Time for a Lightning Round."

"Oh, really, Dad?" Agnes closes her eyes and drops her head practically into her halibut stew.

"Now, Agnes," warns Mom. "You know it's—"

"I know, I know."

My sister is one of the smartest people I know. She's also beautiful, with her short, curly red hair and smooth skin. I can only hope I inherited the same genes. (So far so good.) But, as Auntie Flora would say, Agnes can also serve some major teen sass.

"You go first," Dad says to Agnes, "so you can get it over with." But he's smiling when he says it.

"Fine," she says, and she smiles, too, to let him know she doesn't really mind. "We got to dissect frogs today and it was incredibly smelly and very, very awesome."

Well, the Lightning Round is supposed to be The Most Interesting Thing That Happened To Me Today, and that wasn't quite what we were all expecting, but okay.

"Lovely, dear," says Auntie Flora, spooning up another mouthful of stew.

Agnes and I exchange a look and have to zip our lips closed so we don't laugh.

"Yes, lovely," says Mom and she gives us a look. "Okay, my turn. I went up the elevator with the mayor, and he said, 'Good morning,' and didn't realize that he had a little tissue stuck to his chin where he'd cut himself shaving."

My mom works at the municipal office doing computer stuff, and her stories from work are usually pretty weird IT things, so I have to agree this is a pretty good one, but Dad's on it quickly.

"Good, okay. Not bad. But here's one better." He leans forward and tilts his head, show-off style. "I went to the drive-thru, and the guy ahead of me took so long, he paid for my coffee."

"Oh, good one, John," says Mom, who also frequents the drive-thru for her coffee.

"I know, right? Just drove up with my money out ready to pay and the person at the window said, 'That guy paid for you because he felt bad for taking so long' and that was that." Dad raises his arms like he just won the lottery.

This kind of gives you an idea of what the Lightning Round is all about. So I'm still thinking of something interesting to say as they all turn to me.

"Flora?" says Mom. "What's yours?"

"Oh, I had a song going through my head all day," says Auntie Flora, not looking up, but dipping some bread in her stew.

Okay, it was supposed to be my turn, and sometimes Auntie Flora joins in and sometimes she doesn't, so we all stop and nod at her.

"Earworms," says Agnes, nodding. "Brutal."

"And what was the song?" Mom asks for all of us, and I know we're all wondering if this is going to be one of those times Auntie Flora looks confused and wonders what we're asking, or if she's going to laugh and tell us to never mind, it's not important, or she's going to be completely present and tell us the name of the song.

"It was 'Time is a Fickle Friend,'" she says and

beams a smile around the table at all of us. "My favorite, as you know. And I just couldn't stop humming and singing it all day long. It kept me company and brought back lots of happy memories."

We all relax. It's a good Lightning Round answer.

"It's a beauty," says Dad, and he turns to me. "Maybe you could play that one when you pull out your fiddle later, Flora. Right?"

And I know that's not a just a passing suggestion. It's a request. A "must."

"Of course," I say. "I love that one, too, Auntie Flora."

"And now, last but not least," says Dad, "because the stew is nearly finished and I'm already dreaming about blueberry pie, we need to hear from the other Flora. Take it away. What's your entry for the Lightning Round tonight?"

I'm momentarily stumped. I've already told them about yesterday's Battle of the Bands announcement, and repeats aren't allowed. And school was ordinary, mostly. Except maybe for music class.

Music class.

"Well, Simon, the new kid in our class, chose drums for his instrument in music class. At first, Mrs. García told him that percussion wasn't available because Rudy and Pierre have been the percussion section since Grade Seven, but then Rudy said he'd play trumpet, so Simon DeLuca is going to play drums after all."

It sounds incredibly boring to my ears, but both Mom and Dad sit up in interest.

"Simon DeLuca, son of Theo DeLuca?" Mom asks.

I nod. "I guess. Yup. He's in my class."

"The son of rock royalty," says Dad. "What's he like?"

Hmmm. Tough one. Do I say he turned down Vlad's lunch invitation? And that he keeps to himself and hides behind his long bangs? That he grips his hands together when things aren't going well, such as when Mrs. G. won't let him play the drums? That Kristy thinks he's rude? That Vlad and Bas are willing to cut him some slack? That he knows the weird and wonderful handshake that Rudy did with him after the percussion thing?

"Shy?" Not sure that covers it.

"Is he cute?" Agnes uses her annoying, big-sister teasing voice.

"I don't know." Is he? I haven't thought about it.

"You said drums? He's probably a natural," says Dad. "Probably plays all the instruments. His dad is phenomenal."

He and Mom nod at each other and start talking about Theo DeLuca's greatest hits and where he featured in moments of recent rock history.

I let them. I don't want to talk about Simon DeLuca. I don't even know what I think of Simon DeLuca.

So I push back my chair and grab my empty stew plate. Reach for Agnes's, too. Thankfully, the Lightning Round is over.

But maybe not.

"*Her smile was shy the day we met,*" Auntie Flora starts singing in her pitch-perfect quavery voice as I pick up her plate. "*Her hair blew in the breeze.*"

Singing is not unusual at our dinner table, but Auntie Flora is not usually the first one to start up. Maybe talking about music class got her started. Or maybe it's just the curse of the earworm.

And then Agnes, who just stood up to help clear the breadbasket and butter dish, joins in.

"*We walked down to the rocky shore.*"

Agnes has a beautiful voice. Like Mom, who smiles over at Auntie Flora and sways in her chair as she joins in. "*She gave my hand a squeeze.*"

If my violin was handy, I'd be playing. But my hands are currently full of plates and cutlery, so instead, I sing too. Then Dad joins in. So now there are the five of us singing "Time is a Fickle Friend," in harmony, smiling and laughing together. Typical Parsons dinner table behavior.

"Oh, lovely," laughs Auntie Flora, and it is, so I just forget about Simon DeLuca and music class for a while.

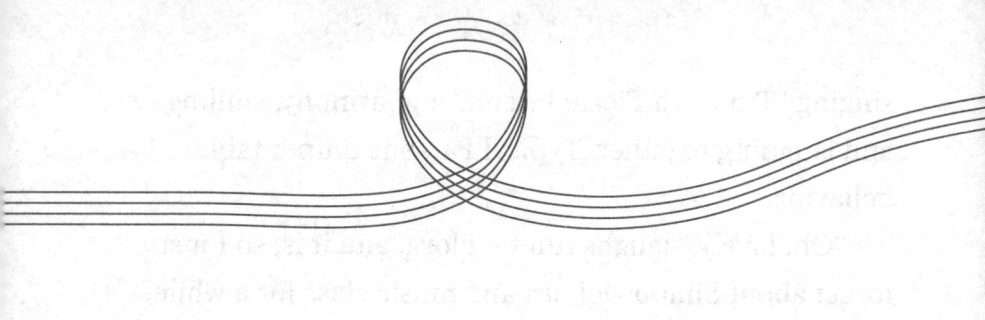

## Chapter 7

VLAD STARTS THE GROUP CHAT JUST AS I'M WRAPPING UP my math homework and thinking about taking my violin—my fiddle—downstairs to play for Auntie Flora.

*Hey. Battle of the Bands. We need a tune.*

Tune? We're a string quartet and our repertoire is pretty much the classics. I like it. No, I love it. The big guns, like Haydn and Mozart and Schubert. And that gorgeous Florence Pryce. Michael Tippet. And maybe my all-time favorite, Finzi's *Romance, Elegy, Prelude*. And yes, okay, we once played something from The Beatles for the Kiwanis Festival showcase. And some *Final Fantasy* last year at a conference Mr. Herndorff got us invited to, and it was cool. But, I don't know.

When I immerse myself and my violin in the classics, I'm lost. Lost in the best way.

So, *tune*? Not quite the word I would use.

*Something fun*, responds Kristy.

*Schubert is fun*, I say.

There's a long pause, which makes me wonder if Vlad and Kristy are chatting quietly to each other. No, they wouldn't do that, would they?

Wait. Would they?

*I was thinking more modern*, says Vlad.

*Me, too.* Kristy. *Let yourself gooooooo, Floooooora!*

She's using her cute persuasion techniques on me. They generally don't work.

*I'm in for whatever.* Bas has joined the conversation and, as usual, is taking the easy road. It's his style, to sit back and let others speak and discuss and argue and decide, and then he just quietly goes along. He's very easy to please. He's the perfect person to have in a group like ours, with Vlad (leader) and Kristy (mouthpiece) and me—well, I'm not sure what I am. But it works, the four of us.

Although, right now I'm not so sure.

*What are you thinking?* I ask.

*Got a million ideas!*

Oh, Vlad. I'm getting nervous now. Punk? Hip-hop?

Alternative? Country? Rock? Golden Oldies?

Newfoundland tunes?

Okay, that would be fine with me. Maybe I'll suggest that...

*Found an arrangement of "Time of Your Life" by Green Day. Also, that* Final Fantasy *soundtrack we did last year.* Vlad has clearly been thinking about this. *That was fun, right?*

*So fun!* Kristy.

*Yup. Sounds good.* Bas, being Bas.

*How about some Bartok or Shostakovich? Or something from this century—loud and weird but still classical stuff?*

Another silence. I finish my last math question and pack my books away, glancing at the screen to see if anyone responds. Nothing. Hmmm.

*Did I scare you all off?*

More silence.

I pick up my violin and tune it quickly. Glance at the clock and see that it's getting late. Auntie Flora will be waiting for me.

*Maybe we should talk in person,* says Vlad.

*Good idea.* Kristy.

*K.* Bas

*Okay.* I'm getting worried now. I can't help but feel

like there's been a conversation behind my back—or screen, or whatever.

*Tomorrow lunch?* Vlad.

We all give his text a thumbs up.

End of chat. And I sit there for a minute feeling— what? Like my friends are ganging up on me? Which is silly. It's just a dumb piece of music we're talking about, not something life-altering, right? But then why does my stomach feel all knotted.

♪

I pick up my violin and head downstairs. And, of course, somewhere between the kitchen and the basement stairs, my violin becomes a fiddle.

"Lots of homework tonight?" Auntie Flora is sitting in her comfy chair watching TV, but she reaches for the remote and turns it off when she sees me.

This is her way of telling me I'm late, but of course, she's smiling.

"Yes, homework and some stuff I had to chat with my friends about." I sit down and lift the fiddle to my shoulder. Do a quick tuning—all good—and look over at her.

She's watching me.

Now, when some people watch you, it means nothing. They're just looking across a table, or a room, and that's all it is.

But when Auntie Flora watches you, with her bright blue eyes slightly narrowed, and her chin tucked down, and her head a bit tilted, like she's thinking—that's when you know she knows.

"What is it, Ducky?"

Yes, she knows just by looking at me that something is on my mind.

No point fighting it, I have learned.

"Your friends." She smiles.

I nod. Sigh.

"Trouble? Real trouble? Or just something that needs your attention."

"It's nothing, really." I shrug. If it's nothing, then why am I feeling this way? "We're just trying to decide which music to play for this contest. The Battle of the Bands, remember I told you about that?"

She nods. "I do. It sounds like such fun. And what is the problem with the music?"

Honestly, the more I think about it, the more I don't want to talk about it. Maybe because I'm feeling more and more like I'm the one with the problem.

"Oh, it's nothing," I wave my bow at her. "Maybe

we'll play some of your tunes. That would be different."

That's it. Smile, lighten the mood.

"That would be lovely," she nods. "So, why don't you practice a few right now."

So that's what I do for ten minutes or so. A slip jig. A crooked tune that she loves. She taps her feet, claps at the end. We laugh. Tonight I seem to be doing it all right.

And then she glances at the clock and shakes her head.

"Oh, my dear, it's getting late. How about one last one. Do you have time?"

"Of course," I say. "What would you like?"

"Something slow," she says. "Maybe something I can sing along to."

Ah. My cue.

I pull the bow across the strings and she starts to sing:

*"Her smile was shy the day we met..."*

I try to press away all my worry and just enjoy the sound of Auntie Flora's voice singing along to my fiddle.

*"Our hearts were joined from that day on,*
*Our time would know no end,"*

I know the song as well as she does, having heard it my entire life from my dad and grandmother. The vinyl recording we have of "Time is a Fickle Friend" always gets pulled out whenever my dad is feeling sentimental. The song was one of the bedtime lullabies my parents sang to Agnes and me back when we needed tucking in.

So I sing along with her as I play.

"*But clouds do come, and waves do roll,*
*And time's a fickle friend…*"

But now, suddenly, I'm hearing it differently. Maybe it's the stuff with Vlad and Kristy and Bas that has me on edge. I'm not sure, because it's not them I'm seeing as I close my eyes and sing along.

It's Simon DeLuca, standing at the front of the class as he tried to get Mrs. García to let him play percussion instead of trumpet or bassoon or whatever. Looking so uncomfortable, with his head down and that long hair falling in front of his face. His hands clenched at his sides.

"*I felt her near, I heard her voice*
*And felt her hand in mine…*
*But always will my Brigus girl*
*Be smiling in my heart.*"

It's like I'm hearing this song for the first time, because the meaning of it comes running at me in a way I've never felt before. I always knew it, but tonight it somehow hits me: it's a song about someone dying. About his wife, his girlfriend, dying.

I play the last chorus without singing, with my eyes closed. Just my fiddle. Auntie Flora isn't singing either.

And when I look over at her, as I pull my bow across the strings on the last long note, I see that she's fallen asleep, still smiling.

# Chapter 8

FIDGETY AND NOT READY FOR SLEEP, I PUTTER AROUND MY room, putting my violin away, packing up my books for school tomorrow, and getting ready for bed.

Where I finally land, a little later than usual, and lie awake for over an hour with my head full of conversation—okay, that text conversation with Vlad, Kristy, and Bas.

*Got a million ideas! Maybe we should chat in person.*

I can't escape the feeling that they're going to gang up on me about our choice of music for Battle of the Bands. Okay, *gang up* might be too strong. We're friends, we're musical teammates. They won't *gang up* on me. And Mr. Herndorff isn't exactly a "Hey Gang, let's try something different" kind of teacher.

But I love our quartet, just the way it is. I love playing all that classical music we play. It makes me feel, I don't know, quiet and strong. It carries me away. It fills me up.

I lie in bed, staring at the ceiling, which is empty and colorless in my dark room. I'm feeling restless, filled up with thoughts that make my stomach churn. And those "Time is a Fickle Friend" lyrics aren't helping. People dying. Like the girl in the song. Like Sophie Andrews's brother, Jackson. Like Simon DeLuca's little sister.

Like Auntie Flora will, too, one day. That thought fills me with—something sad, played in a minor key...

"Stop it!" I whisper to myself in the dark.

♪

Friday morning. Last day of the first week of school.

I'm exhausted.

Okay, it might be because it's the end of the first week of school, with all the people, and the homework, and the changes in routine after a quiet summer, and that's a lot.

Or it might be that I couldn't fall asleep last night, thanks to the thoughts that were racing around my head all night.

Either way, the morning comes too quickly, and I'm fudgy and slow as I go through my morning routines. Shower. Get dressed. Sit at my spot at the kitchen table with a bowl of cereal and the Sudoku, which is always harder on Friday, anyway. Today I'm getting nowhere.

Mom has already left for work, Agnes is—somewhere. Dad is across the table from me, sipping coffee, deep into the Sports section.

"Where's Auntie Flora?" I've been listening for sounds from downstairs, but so far, nothing.

Dad looks up at me, then over his shoulder at the top of the stairs from the basement, listening.

"I can hear her moving around," he says, turning back to me. And maybe he sees something on my face or hears it in my voice. "She'll be up soon, I'm sure."

Last night's keeping-me-awake inner voices are still in my head, I guess. Of course, Auntie Flora is fine down there in her little suite.

And of course, my friends aren't going to gang up on me. We'll talk, we'll laugh, we'll find a great piece to play for Battle of the Bands, and we might even win.

I'm still thinking about my friends and music as I start the fifteen-minute walk to Arden Middle School.

"Hey, Flora!"

I turn around and see Bas jogging to catch up with me. My stomach does a little twist, but I'm pretty sure he can't tell.

"Did you get the Sudoku this morning?" he asks, as usual.

"No, I hardly got anywhere with it."

And the rest of the way we talk about numbers and puzzles, and some new game he has been playing online. I don't have to say much, and right now, this morning after last night, that suits me just fine.

# Chapter 9

"BEFORE WE GET STARTED, I HAVE AN ANNOUNCEMENT," says Mrs. García.

We're in music class—our strings-only music class, this time—and Kristy and I exchange a look.

"The Arden Youth Music Center is going to run a Battle of the Bands competition this fall, for students in two age categories: Middle School and High School. And they're open to auditions from musical groups of all types, all ages. Rock bands, ukulele orchestras, pipes and drums, folk groups. Even string quartets," she pauses and glances around at the four of us, all sitting at the front of our sections, and maybe she's surprised that we don't look more excited, but of course we already knew about this.

The rest of the class is hearing it for the first time, though.

Melina Chan puts up her hand. "Um, Mrs. García? Does it have to be a band? You can't enter as just a solo performer?"

"A band means at least two people, Melina." Mrs. García looks down at some notes in front of her and then back up at Melina, and all of us. "That's what the competition rules say. But if you are a soloist, maybe you could ask someone to join in, on percussion. Or on a harmony instrument?"

Melina plays an amazing Chinese instrument called a zheng, a sort of zither with lots of strings, but she always plays solo. She performs at every school concert and special event and she's brilliant.

"Oh, okay." Melina sighs.

Yes, this Battle of the Bands thing is causing problems all over the place.

"Maybe you can find a collaborator?" Mrs. G. is definitely trying here.

But it's Vlad who speaks up.

"You know..." he starts.

"Yes, Vlad?"

"I was just thinking," he says to Melina, sitting in the first violin section, a few rows behind Kristy and me, "that Brenda, in the band class—do you know her? She plays flute. I bet flute would sound great with your zheng." He shrugs. "Might be fun to try it out."

Melina is shy, and she has a sweet, slow smile that Vlad is getting at full strength right now.

"Thank you," says Melina. "That's a good idea."

"And that's a good idea for all of you, if you're interested." Mrs. García grabs on to Vlad's idea. "Collaborating with one of your classmates in the Band class is a wonderful idea. And I'm sure some of you have electric guitars plugged in at home, too?" She surveys the room.

"I have a boom box," says Robbie Dawes, from the bass section. "Does that count as an instrument, Mrs. G.?"

"I'll leave you to read the rules and follow up with the organizers, Robbie. Now, could everyone pull out your warm-ups folder, please, and we'll do some exercises before turning to today's piece."

And our day continues.

Continues through Music, and History, and right through to lunch, where Vlad, Bas, Kristy, and I find ourselves at a table by the window, spreading out our lunch and, I'm sure, about to launch into our own Battle of the Bands conversation.

And I'm right.

"So. Battle of the Bands," says Vlad before taking a bite of his sandwich. "We're in, right?"

We all nod. No argument there.

Vlad takes a big bite and chews as he looks around at us, so we all wait, because of course he's not going to keep talking with his mouth full.

"But the big question is what we're going to play, right?" Kristy is spooning up yogurt and berries. She doesn't mind eating and talking at the same time.

Vlad nods. We all nod. Here it comes.

"I like the idea of playing something modern," says Kristy. "That *Final Fantasy* piece is a great idea, and we already have the music and everything."

"We need to do some more work on it, of course," says Vlad. "But I like it, too. Shows off the strings. And it's something a bit different that might wow the judges. They'll be expecting our usual stuff and then we hit them with this, right?"

Bas shrugs, nods. "Sure. Sounds good."

Then, the three of them look over at me.

Big inner sigh right now.

I could say: "I don't want to play a twenty-first century game soundtrack. I don't want to be different. I want us to play something from the standard string quartet repertoire. Something Mr. Herndorff thinks we play well. Something we like. Something I love, like Haydn or Mozart or Florence Pryce or Stephen Chatman or..."

I could say this, but I don't.

I chew and swallow, look around at them. My friends. My musical teammates, too. And I can tell they really, really want this and they can't understand why I'm being so negative and difficult. What's going to happen if I don't go along with them? Will they give in, pick one of my pieces, but secretly resent me for it? What if this is the moment that stands between me and them forever...

"You guys pick," I say. "Whatever you want."

Moment's pause.

"You sure?" says Vlad. His eyebrows are practically up to his combed-back black hair, eyes wide. Clearly he wasn't expecting this answer.

None of them were, judging by the expressions on their faces. And why would they, after that chat we had.

I shrug, take another bite. Look around at them. Nod.

"Okay, then!" Vlad practically claps his hands. "We can tell Mr. Herndorff at rehearsal on Tuesday."

"I thought you were all about sticking with the classical stuff," Kristy says to me. Not mean or cranky, but curious.

And because I just don't know how to explain my sleepless night to her—my worrying about them ganging up on me and thinking about people dying, I just shrug.

"It's all music, right? Whatever you guys think. I'm good with it."

"Great," says Vlad. "Good." He bites, chews, smiles, nods.

"Okay. Good!" Kristy nods at us all. "And don't worry, Flora. It has a very classical sound. Very Ravel or one of those Russians. Don't you think?"

Bas smiles. "Oh, yeah. Totally. I love that piece."

Gamer. Of course Bas is going to love that piece.

I just eat my lunch and let them talk as the first violin part of "Lightning's Theme" from *Final Fantasy* starts to swim around in my head. It's okay, really, and it's doing a great job of drowning out all those night thoughts.

Vlad catches my eye and gives me a look. *Right? We're good?*

So I smile, of course. *We're good.* I pull out a container of sliced apple and offer him some.

Decision made. No Battle of the Bands battle. And no, they didn't gang up on me. They didn't need to. Something tells me Auntie Flora would approve.

## Chapter 10

"DON'T EMBARRASS ME, DAD," I SAY AS WE PARK ON THE street outside the school.

"I would never embarrass you, Flora." He pretends to be hurt that I would even suggest it.

"Right."

I don't believe him, because I just spent the entire five-minute drive listening to him and Mom chattering like a couple of YouTube fanatics about the possibility of meeting the famous Theo DeLuca in my classroom at Meet the Teacher Night tonight.

"It's Meet the Creature Night, not Meet the Celebrity Night, right?" Mom tries to sound like she's giving orders, but it's not working.

Yes, it's Meet the Creature Night, which is supposed to be about parents meeting our teachers (who they mostly already know; after all, it's a small school in a small neighborhood), but it usually turns into more of a social gathering.

Mrs. García (who is not only my music teacher but also my homeroom teacher), will make the usual opening remarks about how much she's looking forward to working with our class. Then she'll introduce our other subject teachers who give a little intro. And then she tells us that parents are free to visit with teachers and other parents, and there will be demonstrations in the art room, the gym, and right here in the music room by students, including the Arden Youth Music Center's string quartet.

Once she's done, and all questions have been answered, it becomes a sort of party, with us providing the wallpaper music. (Definition of Wallpaper Music: music performed in the background while no one pays any attention because people don't notice the wallpaper even though it adds some color to the background.)

But, of course, this year is a little different, we all know that there is a new student in our class: Simon DeLuca. The one with the celebrity rock-star dad.

Which makes me the one with the fanboying dad and fangirling mom. I suspect I'm not alone in this.

"I promise we won't ask for autographs," Mom says as we get out of the car.

I'm not sure I can trust them.

Bas and his dad, Mr. Malik, have parked a few spaces up from us and Bas gives me a wave as he gets out of the car and reaches into the back seat for his violin.

"Hi, Flora. Ready?"

"Well," I say with a glance at my parents, who are now walking ahead of us and chattering away with his dad, "I'm ready to listen to Mrs. García's spiel and play some music, but I'm not ready to see my parents go all paparazzi on Simon DeLuca's famous father."

Bas laughs and nods.

"I know, right? Mom was so mad she couldn't come tonight, and Dad promised he'd get her an autograph."

We both shake our heads at that image. I'm sure Bas is seeing the same thing I'm seeing: Simon DeLuca, standing at the front of the classroom, or walking away from us down the hall. This is a guy who clearly does not like to be the center of attention.

Or maybe it's just that he doesn't like people?

And by "people," I mean "us," his classmates.

Also, who knows? Maybe his famous father is exactly the same. If true, there might be a lot of disappointed parents tonight.

"Well, it could be cool to meet a famous rock star, but I will not be asking him for an autograph, and if my parents do anything dumb, I'm moving out," I say.

Agnes would probably love that. She'd have the bathroom all to herself. I think Auntie Flora would miss me, though.

"Who's moving out?"

Vlad moves up beside us, and we bump into each other as we walk up the steps into the school. It's busy and crowded with kids and parents making their way to home rooms, which in our case means the music room.

"Me. If my parents embarrass me," I say.

"And why would your parents embarrass you? They're the coolest parents in school."

Oh, that is so far from the truth. Vlad's parents are so cool to talk to, partly because they have these amazing English accents and always look as if they're about to be photographed for some royalty magazine, and partly because they're just so interested in everything Vlad and his friends (which includes me) are doing. They used to run a dairy farm, but now they are both professors at the university, which might be confusing for students except that Vlad's mom uses her own name. Dr. Baçhman (dad, Department of Agriculture) and Dr. Austen (mom). And no, she's not in the English Literature department, although that would very cool. No, she's a microbiologist and is frequently quoted in the news for her work on food safety and security.

So my parents may be cool, but his parents are next-level cool.

"My parents are not cool," says Bas. "It's okay. Probably better that way. No one asking for autographs and all that."

"Your parents are great," I say, and bump him to show that I mean it. His parents run a furniture store, which means everyone in town has a table, lamp, couch, chair, or other furnishing from the Malik's store on Main Street. They're quiet (unlike my parents) and they donate to all the causes in town. And going to Bas's house means lots of wonderful food, too.

He grins. "Yeah, I know."

We've arrived at the music room and everyone is finding somewhere to sit. Or they're standing around chatting. Mrs. García is up at the front talking to a few parents. There's laughing and a buzz of conversation.

"Feels like a party," says Kristy, who has just put her

viola down on her chair where our quartet arrangement is set up for later.

I see Mom and Dad sitting next to Vlad's parents and they all lean in to say something among themselves. Dr. Austen shakes her head, and I'm sure I just heard her say, "No, we haven't met him yet." All four of them lean back to look around the room.

Looking for rock stars, I'm pretty sure.

"Good evening, everyone," Mrs. García calls out in her teacher voice—the equivalent of that attention-grabbing *one, one, one-two-three* clapping sequence we all remember from kindergarten. "Could you please take a seat and we'll get started? I know everyone's looking forward to refreshments and strolling around the school, but a bit of business first."

The four of us take seats at the back with our classmates because, I mean, this is Grade Eight. Obviously we're not going to sit with our parents.

"At least we don't have homework tonight," Kristy says. "This is way better."

"Is it, though?" Rudy, percussionist-turned-trumpet player, sighs and we all look at him. "What?" he shrugs. "I'd rather be home doing homework than sitting through another one of these 'Here's what we're doing in math this year' and 'You all remember Ms. Chang, our Social Studies teacher?' I mean," Rudy shakes his head. "Why don't we just send our parents to these things and stay home?"

"Doing homework?" Bas jumps in. "Forget it. I'd be on the game console so fast..."

And while this lively conversation is going on, I sit beside Vlad and look over the room to see who's here—and who's not.

And the "who's not" includes Simon DeLuca.

Well, maybe he stayed home. I survey the adults and don't see anyone who resembles an old rock star. But then, famous Theo might have cut his hair and cleaned up into someone who looks like a dad, or a professor. He *is* teaching at the university, after all. But no. I can identify every adult in this room, since we've been doing Meet the Teacher Night at our elementary school, and now at our middle school, since forever.

Simon and his parents are not here.

I look at my parents. They're being good and listening to Mrs. García talk about the subjects on our timetable this year, but then I see my mother glance around again. And she's not the only one.

Honestly, if I were Simon DeLuca and his parents, I'd probably stay away, too.

"I'm just waiting for Mr. LeBrun to join us," Mrs. García

is saying. "He's in the other Grade Eight room down the hall, but I expect him any moment to explain some of the interesting field trips he has lined up, including a trip to the zoo at the end of the school year."

That causes a bit of a buzz, and when someone appears at the door, everyone looks over right away.

But it's not short, bald Mr. LeBrun, with his cool glasses and colorful tie who stands there.

No, it's Simon DeLuca, hiding his eyes behind those long blond bangs, as usual, and a woman who must be his mother. And both of them look like they want to turn around and run.

# Chapter 11

I'M EXHAUSTED, AND I'M GETTING A BIT CRANKY, TO BE honest, because Mom and Dad are talking to Vlad's parents about—what? I'm not sure. Dr. Austen's work? Something at Mom's office? I thought I heard the words "funding" and "Board of Governors," so who knows.

Vlad and I are standing on the sidewalk waiting for them to wrap this up.

"We played well tonight," he says.

I think he's trying to make me feel better about the wait. Auntie Flora would call it "jollying you along." I don't feel at all jolly, just tired. Tired of people talking.

"I guess." I shrug.

"Flora, we played well, and you played really well. Inspired, even. So what's wrong?"

"Thanks for saying that. Nothing's wrong. I'm just tired."

"Is it the Battle of the Bands thing? Playing *Final Fantasy* instead of Mozart?" He looks at me with his head tilted a bit. Something tells me he's still a bit surprised that I gave in so easily on the tune choice last week.

"No, that's fine, really." I wave my hand at him. "Honestly, that just felt like a lot tonight. You know, listening to the same old, same old from Mrs. G. And then playing and having people stop by and ask us to keep going, even when we were ready to stop."

Yes, this happened. Several times. *Oh, please, we just got here. One more, please?* The Grade Sixes and their parents, mostly. Kids who were tiny little people when we left Pauline Johnson Elementary three years ago to start at Arden Middle School. Hard to believe that was us once.

"Yes, it did kind of go on, didn't it." Vlad sighs. "I wanted to go check out the art room. I heard that Mr. Radisson had set up a jewelry-making station. Did you see all those kids with bracelets and stuff?"

"Okay, my man," says someone and we both turn. His dad is holding his arm out and nodding down the street. "Come on, Vlad. Time to head home and get ready for tomorrow."

Goodbyes all round, and they walk away.

"Same goes for us," says Dad, and we start walking in the other direction toward our car. "I'm tired."

"Me, too," says Mom. "And you must be too, Flora. That was a lot of music you guys got through tonight. And it was lovely, by the way. As always."

"Thanks." I yawn a huge yawn.

Dad takes the violin case out of my hand and gives me a quick hug. "We'd better get home and see what trouble Agnes and Auntie Flora have gotten into."

We walk. It's dark on the sidewalk, and most of the cars have gone, just a few families still walking home. This is nice. Peaceful and quiet after all the buzz.

"Excuse me! Hi!" A woman's voice calls out behind us, and we three turn.

It's Simon DeLuca's mom, walking toward us, with Simon trailing along behind her.

"Oh, hi, Petra," calls Mom. "Hi, Simon."

And the reason my mother is on a first-name basis with the wife of the famous rock star is that they already met, in the classroom thanks to Mrs. G. taking control of that awkward moment when Simon and his mother showed up late.

"Oh, please come on in, Mrs. DeLuca, Simon," Mrs. García had waved them in as all eyes turned to them.

Simon was in total pain, I could tell. There's nothing like being the center of attention when you're someone who doesn't want to be the center of attention.

Mrs. DeLuca quickly headed towards the seats Mrs. G. was pointing at and sat down, looking around without looking at anyone directly, the way you do when you're nervous. I could see Mom glancing over a few times, though, trying to make eye contact, probably. Trying to be welcoming.

And when Mrs. G.'s speech was over, my parents and some others made a point of saying hello, the same way they would with any new family. Casual conversation about how they're settling in. No one asked about Mr. Rock Star DeLuca, as far as I could tell—I'm sure Dad was dying to—but by then, Vlad, Bas, Kristy, and I were busy getting set up to perform and I was distracted, so who knows?

I did look up once and see Simon watching us, though. Interested? Bored? Not sure.

So now here we are, standing on the dark sidewalk as Mrs. DeLuca and Simon walk toward us. She has car keys in her hand, so they must be that SUV I can see further down the block behind our car.

"Sorry, I didn't mean to startle you," Mrs. DeLuca says. "I just wanted to catch up and say hi again, and thanks for being so welcoming tonight."

"Don't be silly!" Mom goes into full welcoming mode. "Walk along with us, Petra."

"Nothing like making an entrance, huh?" Mrs. DeLuca is laughing at herself now. She has long hair tied up in a fluffy, sticking-out bun kind of thing, and a wardrobe that Agnes would kill for—a tunic dress and leggings, boots, perfectly fitted and faded jean jacket. And a necklace and several bracelets, not to mention a rock of a sparkly ring on the hand holding the keys.

In other words, she is totally Vogue while my parents belong in the flyer from that store in the mall that always has sales.

Dad is still carrying my violin, but he drops his arm from around my shoulder and moves along with the two moms.

"So, what do you think of the neighborhood, Petra?" he asks.

Simon and I are now following them. Yes, side by side. Walking down the sidewalk, listening to the adults. If this was any other kid from school, by now we'd be talking about stuff—the whole event we just endured at school, homework, that future trip to the zoo. Anything.

But I'm not sure where to start with this kid. He doesn't seem to like anyone—oh, he might like Rudy. I did see them talking for a few minutes tonight before Simon followed his mom out of the music room, I guess to check out the gym, or art room. There was that percussion-trumpet thing in music class, and the handshake. Definitely an icebreaker.

But all I'm feeling here is ice.

"Our house is on Major Street," Mrs. DeLuca is saying. "It's cozy, and that's really all we wanted."

"That's not far from us," Mom says. "Beautiful old houses there. And the trees!"

"I know, it's lovely. And there's a perfect attic space for Theo's stuff. You know, electronics and instruments. The stuff he needs for this course he's teaching at the university."

"Recording equipment?" Dad asks. *Oh, Dad. Your fanboy is showing.*

I must make a sound, because beside me, Simon says, "It's okay. Everybody wants to know that."

I glance over and he looks at me, and shrugs.

"Everybody wants to know if he's going to record something new."

"Oh," I say. I can hardly believe this guy is actually talking to me, so it takes a moment to process something to say. "Is he?"

Simon shakes his head. "Probably not."

Our parents are laughing together and saying goodnight as we arrive at our car, so this conversation is over. I'm a bit relieved, to be honest.

"Come on, Simon," his mom turns and puts out an arm towards him. "Let's get you home."

"Yup, okay." He starts walking away, and then stops, turns back to me.

"You guys sounded really good tonight," he says.

I look up at him in surprise because a compliment, something nice, is about the last thing I expected to hear, but he's already turned away to catch up with his mom.

"Thank you!" I call after him.

He doesn't turn around, but he gives a wave. I guess to let me know he heard me.

"Weird kid," I say. But not loud enough for anyone to hear.

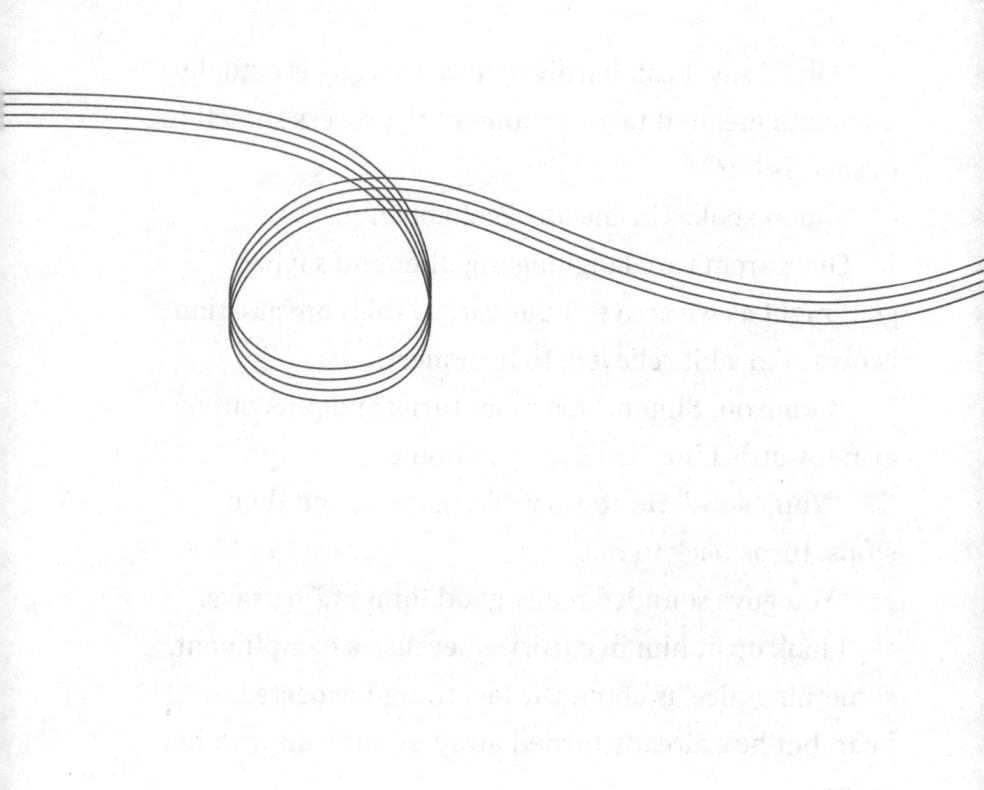

# 𝄞 Chapter 12

TODAY, FRIDAY, IS OUR JOINT BAND-STRINGS CLASS.

It's not my favorite class, to be honest.

Yes, music all day, every day, works for me. But this is different.

I can tell that some of my classmates just don't get it. And they don't care that they don't get it. Everybody has to take music in Grade Eight, and everybody has to learn an instrument, at least until they can run away screaming from it in high school.

The problem is that playing a musical instrument may have many benefits (as Mrs. G. always says when parents are around, and even sometimes in class when things aren't going well), but playing a musical instrument can be hard, too. It's not easy. And for some people, it's not fun. And that is very clear in our class, sometimes.

Back in Grade Four we were introduced to recorders, which I heard Avril Dupont's dad describe as "torture sticks" and I could almost sympathize. A recorder played badly by a room full of ten-year-olds IS torture. (Played well, there is nothing sweeter, as Vlad and I proved when we won the gold medal at Kiwanis in Grade Five.) Yes, recorders can be bad, but just let me say, there is nothing that will make you squirm like the sound of violins, violas, cellos, and basses being played by people who don't get it and don't care. It's scary, actually.

And then there's band class, with all those clarinets and saxophones and their squeaking reeds. Now *that* is the definition of torture.

It was a shock for Vlad, Bas, Kristy, and me when we arrived in music class in Middle School, that first week of Grade Six, fresh from our years building our string quartet skills at the Arden Youth Music Center.

I have to admit, though, our classmates have come a long way. And there are definitely some real musicians in our class. Melina being one of them. And Rudy, although I haven't actually heard him play trumpet yet. And others, of course. We sound pretty good, most of the time.

But I still have to bite my lip and make sure I'm not making a face when Avril and Meghan, who sit behind Bas in the second violin section, don't play in tune. Or Brent squeaks his clarinet all through a piece. It kills me, but I manage to do it.

Because to show how much it bothers me would be rude, and I know exactly what Auntie Flora would say about that.

So here I am, Friday morning, in music class, ready to be a good classmate. A good bandmate. Ready to let the flat/sharp strings and dragging tempo and squeaking reeds do their thing. It's just the way music class goes, right? I will endure it.

It turns out, I'm in for a surprise.

"We'll start with scales this morning, everyone," says Mrs. García. "After a long break over the summer, you all need to be reminded where to put those fingers and what tempo means. Right?"

Inner groan heard silently throughout the room. Scales are so boring.

Well, they can be boring. They can also be intense, like when Vlad and I race each other through C, C-sharp,

D, E-flat, E—and onward up the chromatic scales. And this is something we would never, ever try in music class.

"We'll start with C. Four beats on each note going up, repeat at the top and come back down," says Mrs. García. "And percussion section? Feel free to range through the instruments, but please follow my baton and keep a steady beat, like this." She demonstrates her up and down and across 4/4 baton swing. Mrs. G. dreams of being in front of a big orchestra one day, I can tell. She really makes that baton work.

Vlad catches my eye, raises his eyebrows, and mouths, *"Cowbell."*

We can only hope. I glance back at Simon and Pierre and see they both have drumsticks in their hands, so I guess we're going with plain old toms and snare to start with. Maybe we'll get some cymbals at some point?

"All right. Starting on C. I'll count you in. One, two, three, four." Baton in motion, and so are we.

*C C C C, D D D D, E E E E, F F F F, G G…*

Wait. What was that?

Everyone's eyes swivel to the back of the room, to the percussion section, because Simon DeLuca has just added some beats in syncopation. Nothing big, just a gentle change in texture, an added cymbal, and we all heard it.

Simon has his head down, hiding behind his bangs again, of course. Pierre is keeping it simple on the snare, but he looks over at Simon as if he's waiting for something big to happen. Maybe we all are.

Mrs. García looks at Simon, but she keeps the baton moving and doesn't say anything other than calling out the notes.

We finish the C scale with a gentle *ting* on the cymbal. Unexpected, but I see everyone smiling. Even Mrs. G.

"Okay, then. Let's move on to G."

This time she doesn't call out the notes, which is unfortunate because a number of people forget the F-sharp. But it doesn't matter. Someone always forgets that extra stretch on the A string or change of fingering on those holes or valves. We just keep going. We keep going to the beat of the drums.

And the drums are starting to make themselves heard. And felt.

Yes, Simon and Pierre are adding some definite percussion vibes to our scales warmup, and everyone is starting to feel it, including Mrs. G.

Vlad and I exchange glances. *Is she SMILING?*

She is. And she's not alone. I glance around and see everyone's eyes darting to the back to watch Simon and Pierre. Wait! Did I just hear a *triangle?*

I did! A quick glance reveals Pierre has given up on the cymbal and is rocking a triangle. He and Simon are grinning at each other with that expression that rock band drummers get. They're into it. Mouths open. Counting and not counting.

Simon's drum kit is getting more of a workout now. More beats, more syncopation. And Pierre's triangle is sending out a steady 2-and-4 beat, and it's awesome.

"Stay on the G scale!" Mrs. García calls out. "Again!"

Yes, everyone is into it now, which is easy for us string players. It's easy to smile and laugh when you don't have an instrument stuck in your mouth. Rudy actually stops playing his trumpet (and he's a natural, so he's doing great at it) and calls out "Mrs. G.! We're rocking this!" And that makes everyone laugh and only the strings keep the scale going for a few beats until everyone gets their mouthpieces back in.

"Cowbell!" Vlad calls this out while doing that head-banging thing that rockers do. Very easy for cellists. "More cowbell!"

Everyone—yes, even Mrs. García—laughs and there's some foot stomping in support.

I glance back at Simon again to see what he's going to do. I mean, he strikes me as that kid who doesn't like anyone to tell him what to do. A loner, maybe. (And why not? New school, famous father, sad family history. I get it, even if Kristy doesn't.)

But right now he's grinning at Pierre as they keep playing while changing positions. Pierre has dropped the triangle and is sitting at the drum kit so he can thump the bass drum and the toms. Big, hard, solid beats on 2 and 4. Simon skirts around beside him while keeping one drumstick on the snare and drops the other one to reach for—yes, the cowbell.

And that's how we play our final G scale. We finish with one big crash on the bass drum followed by a final clang on the cowbell and the whole class cheering and clapping.

"So awesome!" Rudy calls out above the noise.

"Can we do that again, Mrs. García?" Avril Dupont is laughing. And Avril is the most serious girl I know and she rarely laughs, so this is something.

Even quiet, shy Melina is jiggling a little while she smiles and looks around.

"Percussion section," says Mrs. García, looking at the two boys at the back. We all wait because, who knows? Teachers sometimes don't like it when students go rogue in their classroom. And Simon and Pierre definitely went rogue here.

"Boys?" She nods her head, smiling a little. I think we're okay here. "That was the most fun running scales I've had in a long, long time. Thank you for being so creative."

We all start to clap, maybe from relief that Simon and Pierre aren't going to get yelled at, but also because we all agree.

"Your choreography while changing positions was amazing and your musical improvisation was sublime," she says. And then she tilts her head and raises her eyebrows a little. "But, let's just say, don't get used to doing that, okay?"

"Okay," says Pierre, and he looks over at Simon. "It sure was fun though."

Simon puts out his fist for the bump thing. No fancy handshakes this time.

"And Simon?" Her face is serious now.

The room goes quiet. I glance back at him, but he doesn't show any emotion. He's sitting on the stool behind the drums, head tilted a bit so his bangs fall forward, no expression on his face.

"I hope you're putting together something for the Battle of the Bands."

And much to everyone's amazement, he smiles. It transforms his face completely, and I know I'm not the only one who notices. Kristy catches my eye, eyebrows raised.

"I'm thinking about it," he says. "Thanks."

"Good," says Mrs. García, back to business. "Now, class, let's pull out that score I gave you in our class last week. Some Vivaldi to kick off the year." She looks around at us. "And it's in C, too, so you should be all warmed up."

As I get ready to enjoy the familiar Baroque classic being destroyed by our music class, I think to myself how much I'd love to play in a band with someone who can do what Simon DeLuca just did.

## 𝄞 Chapter 13

"AND DID YOU DANCE?"

Auntie Flora, Agnes, and I are sitting around the firepit in our backyard on Saturday after supper. We're all wearing extra layers, and Auntie Flora even has one of her famous nan blankets draped over her knees, all those multi-colored granny squares crocheted by her own hands and stitched together. We have about five of them, all different sizes. It's how she uses up all the bits and pieces of yarn that she collects from her other projects. Yes, Auntie Flora is a hard-core knitter and crocheter.

It's September, and it's chilly out here, but cozy, too, with the fire going and the sun just down. There's still light in the sky, though. Enough light to see Agnes's face. She's staring into the flames, smiling a little.

"Yes, Auntie Flora, we danced."

"That's good, then."

Agnes has been telling us about her *not-a-date* last night with a boy named Cedric. According to Agnes (after some prodding by Auntie Flora and me) the fish and chips were good, the band was great, the crowd was fun, and the room was full. It sounds to me as if the not-a-date was a success.

Auntie Flora turns to me and says, "You know what would be perfect right now, Ducky?"

"S'mores?" I drag my eyes away from the fire.

"No, Ducky, I was thinking a tune would be lovely right now."

"A tune?"

"Brings back memories of times we had at Joe Penney's place, up the road from us on The Bay. After supper, before it got dark and the fisherman had to turn in, we'd have a little gathering around the fire at Joe's, and there would be tunes and singing and recitations."

"My mom used to tell me about that," Dad says, arriving with a camp chair and joining us. "She was little, but she remembered. You and Joe and some of the others, singing and telling the old stories."

"Oh, yes, your mother was a little girl and she wanted to be right in there with the rest of us," Auntie Flora nods. "She's a one, your mom."

To clarify, Auntie Flora is my grandmother's aunt, which makes her my father's great-aunt, and my great-great-aunt. If my Grandma was here right now, we'd have four generations sitting around this fire. Yes, it's a little complicated.

"Did I hear you ask for some tunes?" Mom arrives, carrying my violin case. Or maybe it's a fiddle case right now.

So that's how we came to be sitting there in the backyard, me playing tunes very quietly with the mute on my bridge. Mom and Dad and Agnes and especially Auntie Flora smiling into the fire and tapping and head-nodding along to "Frank Stamp's" and "Tom Lake's" when we hear a voice behind us say, "Hello? We were just passing by and heard the music."

I stop playing and we all turn to see Petra DeLuca smiling at us from the shadows, with Simon beside her, looking embarrassed. And behind them is a tall, extremely thin man with gray hair tied back in a ponytail.

"Um, hi!" Dad stands up and nearly knocks his camp chair over, which tells me everything I need to know.

Theo DeLuca, famous rock star, just appeared in our backyard.

♪

So now I'm sitting next to Simon DeLuca and we're not talking to each other.

Okay, I don't mean, we've decided not to talk to each other, like after a fight or something. No, it's much simpler than that.

Dad got chairs down from the deck so there would be enough for everyone, and then he did the assigned seating. Of course, he wanted to make sure that he was sitting next to Mr. DeLuca, and Mom very quickly got Mrs. DeLuca into the chair between her and Auntie Flora—yes, my chair.

"Let's let Petra sit here, okay, Flora? How about you and Simon take those two chairs to the other side of the fire."

So here we are. Simon and me sitting side-by-side. And Agnes across the firepit, beside Auntie Flora, giving me the eye. *Sitting with the rock star's kid, Flora?*

It's all very neighborly and normal, just the kind of thing my parents love. Friends dropping in for an unexpected kitchen party. Only this time it's in the back yard, in the dark, around the firepit.

"It's so nice to finally meet you, Theo," says Dad oh-so-smoothly, not giving away that he's a bit star-struck. (And I only know this because I caught him and Mom giving each other a *Wow-is-this-happening?* look after he and Mr. DeLuca had introduced themselves and sat down.) "I guess it takes a while to settle into a new city, right? Are you liking the neighborhood?"

"Nice neighborhood. Nice to meet some neighbors, yeah," says the famous rock star who just looks like someone's dad. Or grandfather maybe. He seems older than most of the dads I know. He looks a little tired.

"A stroll after supper is always nice at this time of year," Mom says. Which is funny because she and Dad never go for strolls. I don't catch Agnes's eye because she might be thinking the same thing as me and we'd probably laugh.

"We love this neighborhood," says Mrs. DeLuca.

And the moms are off, talking about houses and gardens and the differences between here and the DeLuca's old place.

I take a quick look at silent Simon. He's watching his mother and sort of smiling.

Okay, smiling is good. It means he's happy, right?

"So, that was cool, what you and Pierre did in music class yesterday," I say. "Jazzing up the scales, I mean."

He shrugs, but he's still smiling, and he glances over at me.

"Sometimes I can't help myself," he says.

"I know what you mean," I say, thinking of the times Auntie Flora has given me that look, or tapped her walking stick on the floor, to remind me to slow down, to play the notes the way the old fiddlers play them.

"You sounded good," he says. He nods at my violin case, now lying on the grass behind my camp chair. "When we walked by, we could hear you, and my mom said we had to find out who was playing. Because she knows tunes like that."

Well, that's interesting. "Your mom? Your mom knows Newfoundland tunes?"

He shakes his head. "No, no. Not Newfoundland tunes. Appalachian. She grew up in North Carolina."

Ah. Similar, but not the same. Music the settlers brought over hundreds of years ago from Scotland and England and Ireland.

"Does she play?"

"Nah." He shakes his head and glances at me. Then he pushes his bangs out of his eyes and looks over at his mom, now talking to Auntie Flora. "She used to hum them.

The tunes, I mean. Sing them. Just the notes. Sometimes with words. She..." but he stops.

I look over at him and now he's staring at the fire.

"She used to sing to Grace," he says. "My little sister."

His little sister who died.

I should say something. Auntie Flora says death is a part of life, and that sharing it with people is showing kindness. I should say, *I'm so sorry,* but I don't know how he'll react. And did anyone hear him just say that? (A quick glance around. No, Dad is talking and Mr. DeLuca is looking at him and nodding. Mom, Mrs. DeLuca, and Agnes are laughing at something Auntie Flora just said.)

So, it's me and Simon and what he just said about his little sister. *Now, Flora,* I tell myself, and just as I'm getting the words ready, Dad calls over, "Hey, Flora. Get that fiddle out. Theo says he'd love to hear some of our favorite tunes."

"Oh, yes, please," says Mrs. DeLuca. "I grew up with fiddle music. I'd love to hear some of your tunes." She turns to Auntie Flora, and adds, "Your Newfoundland tunes."

And the moment is lost.

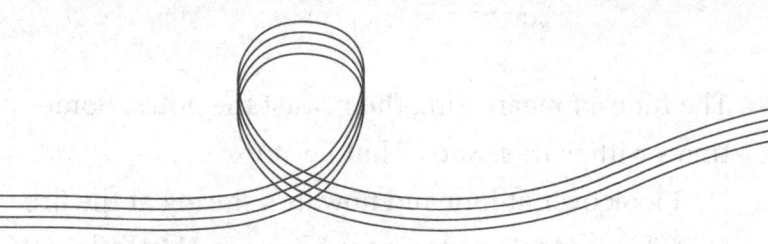

# Chapter 14

"HE HAS A PONYTAIL? THAT'S COOL."

Kristy and I are walking over to Vlad's house for a Sunday afternoon rehearsal. Vlad's idea, not Mr. Herndorff's. Vlad is very excited about the whole Battle of the Bands thing and messaged us all this morning.

*You guys free for some practice this afternoon? My house?*

And then when we three didn't reply right away (in my case because I was still sleeping), he added, *My mom is baking cookies.*

So Kristy and I are on our way to Vlad's, and we'll meet Bas there. And there will be cookies.

I'm telling Kristy about the unexpected visit last

night and she has fixated on Mr. DeLuca's ponytail. This is fine with me, because I really don't want to go into all the details about my conversation with Simon, or how much his mother loved the tunes. Much toe-tapping and head-nodding in time to "Parson's Pond Jig," and Petra's huge smile, and her "Oh, my Lord, Theo, doesn't this take you back to the Charlotte County Fair?" and his reply, in his growly voice, "Sure does, honey."

And I'm not going to tell Kristy about how Mrs. DeLuca said, "Theo knows some tunes. Play one, honey."

"How about some 'Cumberland Gap'?" he said, and then played it on my fiddle—my violin—and it was amazing.

"Yes, he has a ponytail and a really low growly voice, you know? He sounds more like some old country singer," I say.

"Probably beat up his throat yelling out all those rock songs," says Kristy. She's the youngest in her family, with three older brothers, and her parents are older than mine, so their family music library stretches way back. I've seen vinyl from the '70s lying around in their living room.

"Probably."

"What did Simon do? Did he talk or anything?" She gives me a sideways look, as if she expects a definite *No*.

"He was quiet, but yes, he talked."

"Really? About what?"

I guess I could tell her how he talked about his mom, and the tunes she used to sing to his little sister, but I don't want to talk about dead little sisters with Kristy, or anyone, so I just say, "We talked about that fun we had playing scales the other day in music class." Which is true.

"That was pretty awesome. And it was cool that Mrs. G. didn't freak out about him and Pierre getting all crazy. I mean, that cowbell!"

We arrive at Vlad's house, which means I can change the subject.

"So, *Final Fantasy*, here we come," I say, and try to sound enthusiastic.

"Hey, Flo, it'll be great," says Kristy as we go up the porch steps. "I know you'd rather be sticking to the classical stuff. But we sound good, you know? And Vlad's really excited about doing something different."

"I know. It's all fine," I say.

And I mean it. It *is* all fine. This fun Battle of the Bands idea, which is new. Getting to play music with my friends.

"You're here!" Vlad must have seen us coming because he throws open the door and welcomes us as if he hasn't seen us for ages. "Come on. Cookies first. Then rehearsal."

We run through the *Final Fantasy* score in our music folder, and it sounds pretty good, even though we haven't played it for almost a year.

"Sounds good," Vlad says. "But maybe we need to jazz it up a little, make it stand out more. I mean, it *is* a contest, and we want to show off a bit, right?"

"Right," says Kristy. "Maybe we could mess with the rhythm a little? Make it sound a bit less 'classical'?"

"Cowbell," says Bas, and of course we all laugh.

We talk some more, practice a couple of other pieces in our folder—we pick my favorite Haydn, a little Dvorak, because we need to keep our usual classical pieces ready for festival season in the spring, too. And after a lot of cookies (of course!), we pack up and head home.

Where there's a surprise waiting for me.

"You have a visitor," calls Mom from the kitchen as I come in the front door.

A visitor?

I carry my violin into the kitchen and see—

Simon DeLuca sitting at the table with Auntie Flora.

## Chapter 15

"UM, HI," I SAY.

"Hi," he says.

His bangs are brushed a bit to the side today, so I can see his eyes. He looks at me, looks down, looks at Mom, looks down, looks at me. Looks at the mug in front of him and picks it up. Takes a gulp.

Yes, Simon DeLuca is sitting in my kitchen drinking tea with Auntie Flora.

"We've been having the most wonderful chat," Auntie Flora says. "About boats."

*Boats?*

"Oh, that's nice," I say.

He looks at me and shrugs. "Ferries."

"Fairies?" Now I'm confused.

"Oh, Flora, you make me laugh," Auntie Flora waves her hand at me. "Get yourself some tea and sit here with us. We're talking about ferries, Ducky, the boats that take you across the water."

"Oh, *ferries*. Got it."

"Here you go." Mom puts my tea down in front of me in my favorite mug. "How was practice?"

"Good." I sip. "Thanks, Mom." My tea is perfect. Strong, sweet, lots of milk.

This is all helping me avoid looking at Simon sitting there. Why? Why is he here?

"You were practicing?" he says to me. Conversation with Auntie Flora about ferries is on hold, I guess. "With Vlad and those guys, you mean?"

I nod. Sip.

He nods. Sips. He puts his mug down and takes a breath like he's getting ready to say something big. But all he says is, "So, was this for the Battle of the Bands thing?"

"Yeah. We're working on a gamer music thing, just to be a bit different, you know?" I hope I sound convincing to him because I sure don't sound convincing to myself.

"Well, cool." He takes another sip.

I wonder what Mom and Auntie Flora think of this conversation. It's so weird to have Simon here. I mean, I hardly know him, and he hasn't exactly been very friendly at school. But maybe when you sit at a firepit and tell someone that your mom used to sing to your little sister, who is now dead...well. Maybe that changes things.

I tell myself to be nice. He's here for a reason and he will tell us when he's ready.

Wait, *why* is he here? Why would he come to our house and sit in our kitchen drinking tea and talking about ferries with Auntie Flora while waiting for me to come home from practice?

"The ferry from North Sydney to Port aux Basques can be quite a choppy ride," Auntie Flora says, as if the last few awkward minutes of weird conversation between Simon and me didn't happen. She just picks up where she left off. "More than one green-faced tourist, I can tell you. And goodness, we had to dodge icebergs on the way to Fogo Island one time, I remember. Back when we went to visit an old school friend who'd moved up there to marry a fisherman and make quilts. I think she still runs a quilting store there."

Auntie Flora smiles at Simon and me, takes a sip of her tea. We nod back. Take sips of our tea, too. I wonder if he knows I'm trying to figure out why he's here.

"So, Simon," says Mom, to the rescue. "You said you had something to ask Flora?"

*Awkward, Mom.* But helpful, too.

Simon wraps his hand around his mug and looks down at the tea, and then up at me. The bangs have fallen down over his eyes again. (How can he stand it? It must tickle.)

"Yeah, so, I was wondering," he says, "would you be interested in joining my band? For the Battle of the Bands thing?"

"Oh, isn't that a lovely idea," says Auntie Flora.

*No, Auntie Flora, not a lovely idea.*

"Um," I say. It's all I can manage.

"I know you're already in the quartet thing, with your friends, but I checked with Mrs. García, and people can be in more than one band, if they want, and I have this idea for a band, and I just thought you might be good at it."

I admit it. I'm staring at him with the thought *Are you kidding?* going through my head.

"Um…"

"Oh, Flora, go on, then," says Auntie Flora. She turns to Simon. "And what kind of a band are you thinking of?"

He looks at her. Looks at me.

"Retro rock," he says. "You know, like classic vinyl. Journey. Bon Jovi. Peter Gabriel. ACDC. Quiet Riot."

Auntie Flora, Mom, and I all look at him with exactly the same expression on our faces. The expression that says, *What?*

"Look, I know it sounds weird, right? But my dad played a lot of garage rock, old rock, he can play anything. And I've been playing around with it, too, mostly playing bass guitar, though."

He's getting warmed up and even though I'm not quite following, I have the feeling he's talking about something he knows a lot about.

"You need a guitarist," says Mom. "Is that it?"

Simon nods at her, and then he looks at me. He looks completely different from the boy at school. The boy who won't sit with anyone, who hides behind his bangs, or at the back of the music room behind his drums.

"Yeah, the band needs a guitarist, but…"

"But I don't play guitar." Surely he knows this.

"But you can play those riffs, the solos, the wild runs and stuff. They'd sound amazing on violin. I've heard them. Dad played with some guys once and they brought in this guy on a violin, an electric violin, and he could outplay the other guys on those parts, and it was amazing."

He stops and looks around at us. Does he know that he just transformed right in front of us? He leans on the table with his hands waving around while he talks. He's smiling, excited by his brilliant idea, and he looks right at me.

"You could so do it," he says, and nods his head. "You could. And it would be so cool and so different, and we'd have a great shot at winning this contest."

"Um." I'm trying to process this new Simon. And picture myself playing rock violin.

I also try to picture myself telling the Arden String Quartet that I'm joining another band.

"I don't know," I say. "I mean, there's only one of me, and I'm already playing with Vlad and Bas and Kristy, and we'll be practicing a lot, and..."

"Look, I know it sounds kind of crazy," he says. "I know it's probably something you've never done before. So how's this? How about you come over to my house. Bring your violin, and we'll try some stuff. My dad has some recordings and he can show you what I'm talking about."

"What, now?"

"Sure. Now. Why not?"

I look over at Mom, who has been keeping very quiet over there by the sink, and she raises her eyebrows at me and shrugs. *Why not?*

Oh, great, thanks a lot, Mom.

"You'll have to tell me how it goes," says Auntie Flora. "Tonight, when you come down to play tunes. Maybe you'll have some new ones to play for me."

"Oh, I don't think they're those kind of tunes, Auntie Flora." I look at Simon and he's grinning.

"You play tunes every night?"

"Every night," says Auntie Flora. "My Flora comes downstairs and we visit all the good ones, right, Ducky? You'll have to join us, Simon." She turns to him. "We'll find you some spoons to play, won't we?"

"I would love that, Mrs. Parsons," he says to her. And then he looks at me again and shrugs. "So, what do you say?"

"Off you go, Flora." Auntie Flora pushes herself up from the table and looks at me. "I want to hear how you make out with those new tunes of his. Sounds like such fun. Go on, then." And she makes a shooing motion with her hand as she heads to the stairs. "I'm off to watch the baseball. Call me when it's dinner time, Sylvia," she says to Mom.

That's Auntie Flora, giving orders.

Which is how I find myself walking to Simon DeLuca's house to play rock violin.

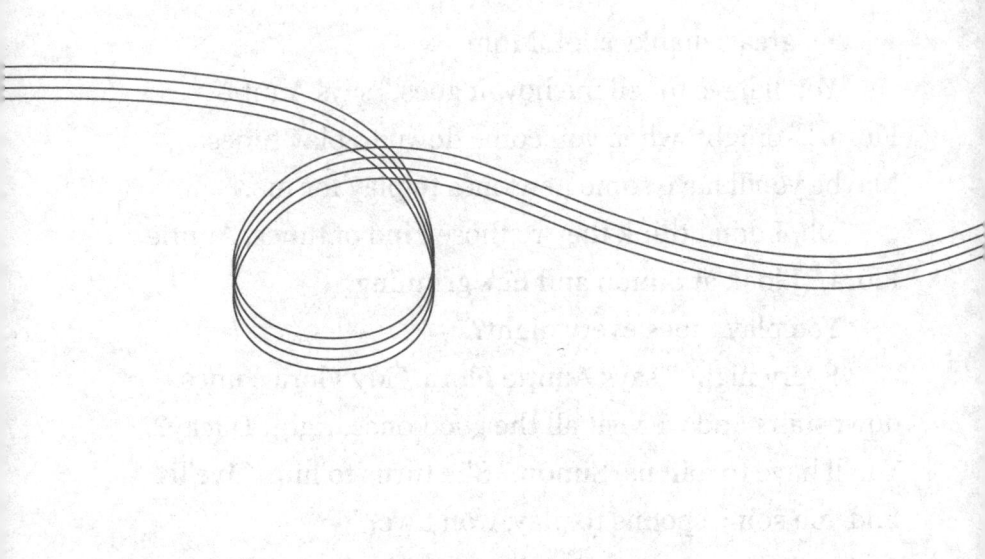

# Chapter 16

SIMON'S HOUSE IS A COUPLE OF BLOCKS AWAY, SO IT doesn't take long to get there. This is a good thing for two reasons.

First, I'm worried someone will see us, like Vlad, or somebody's mom, driving by. And they'll go home and say to Vlad (or Bas, or Kristy, or one of my classmates), "I just saw Flora Parsons walking along the sidewalk with that new boy with the long hair." And what kind of conversations would that lead to?

Second, after all that excited talking at my kitchen table about his Battle of the Bands idea, Simon isn't really much of a talker. This means we walk along in silence, mostly. It feels awkward and weird.

I decide to channel my inner Auntie Flora and start a conversation. But just as I'm getting ready to ask more about his Battle of the Bands idea, he turns in at a red brick house with a porch, almost a twin of our house.

"Home sweet home," he says as I follow him up the sidewalk.

My stomach gives a little twist. Why am I nervous? I've met his parents—his mom a couple of times, now. She's nice. His dad just seemed like a quiet guy, kinda like Simon, at the firepit the other night. A quiet guy who can play "Cumberland Gap" and "Soldier's Joy" really fast on the fiddle. And who can be found on the internet, both good and bad. Famous.

My stomach gives another twist. Why am I even doing this?

Because Auntie Flora thought it sounded like fun and practically told me to go. Maybe I need to have a talk with Auntie Flora. Or maybe I should stop listening to her? No, that would be impossible.

"Well, hello!"

We've just come in the door and Mrs. DeLuca is already coming toward us from the kitchen, a big smile on her face.

"Hello, Mrs. DeLuca." Manners, manners, manners. Drilled into Agnes and me since birth.

"See? Didn't I tell you, Simon? I told you Flora would be interested."

Mrs. DeLuca has a cool accent, like I've heard on country music videos. I guess that's the Charlotte, North Carolina, thing. Very soft and flowy. I could listen to her talk all day.

And then I hear what she just said. *I told you Flora would be interested.* Which means they were talking about me.

"Mom," says Simon in that voice we kids use to tell our parents it's time to stop talking, but she just ignores him, of course.

"It's nice of you to help Simon out with his band idea for this contest," she says to me. "It sounds like such fun, and Simon doesn't know a lot of kids at school yet. And after our visit the other night, we got talking and I said, 'That Flora would help you out,' and I was right, because here you are."

"Um, yup," I say.

"Where's Dad?" Simon jumps in before she can say another word. "Upstairs?"

She nods. "Where else? You going up?"

"Is that okay?"

"Of course, honey. Up you go. Kick him out and tell him I need some help down here."

"Okay. Come on." He looks over his shoulder at me and I follow him upstairs.

We keep going up, past the bedrooms, up to the room at the top of the stairs. We have the same room at our house, a joint office that my parents use when they work from home. I only go up there to use the printer, but it's a nice space, with a tall window at the front, a couple of side windows, and desks against each wall.

The DeLuca's office is a bit different though.

We come through the door and stop. And I feel my heart start to beat faster.

Guitars. Maybe five of them, hanging from stands. Two electronic keyboards. A big djembe and what looks like a miniature drum kit. A bookshelf full of books and smaller percussion instruments, some I don't even recognize. Electronic sound boards and computer screens surrounding a desk. And curtains hanging from rods on the ceiling, most of them drawn together and out of the way.

The room is packed full of music, and right in the middle, sitting at the desk and wearing headphones, is Simon's dad.

He catches sight of us as we come through the door and swivels around on his chair.

"Hey." That's all he says as he gives us a wave and slips the headphones off to sit around his neck.

"Hey, Dad," says Simon.

"Brought your fiddle." Mr. DeLuca nods at me. "Great."

I nod back. This is a man of few words. I'm a girl of few words, too, right now, standing here holding my violin in what is clearly a famous person's music room.

"Hey, Dad, can you cue up that Ozzy Osbourne we were talking about?" Simon turns to me and nods at my violin. "Maybe you could listen to this, and give it a try? I mean, I'm not sure this is a song we'd want to play, but it'll give you an idea of how a violin can play licks."

*Licks.* Can I play rock-style licks? Well, we're about to find out.

I put my violin case on the floor, snap it open, and check the tuning while Mr. DeLuca is on the computer searching what looks like a playlist.

And then, as I prop my violin loosely under my chin and tighten the bow, the music starts. Loud music, rock music.

"'Crazy Train,'" Simon leans over so I can hear him better. "Classic."

It is a classic, and I'm sure I've heard it before, probably when Dad puts his classic rock station on the car radio.

It's pretty hard-core rock, all right. Simon and his dad are both doing a bit of head nodding in time to the notes marching out in an intense rhythm, and I start to feel it, too. Not just the rhythm, but the pattern of notes. Up and down, like a broken arpeggio. Like a fingering exercise. Like—Mozart?

No, of course not like Mozart. I mean, this is rock music, right?

But I hear it so clearly, the pattern. And the rhythm just swallows me up. Before I know it, my violin is secure under my chin, my fingers are on the fretboard, the bow is on the strings, and I'm playing along.

Yes, I'm playing Ozzy Osbourne on my violin.

Simon and his dad both look at me. They have the exact same expressions on their faces as they nod along to the beat: *You get it*.

Yes, I get it. But not only do I get it...

I LOVE it.

# Chapter 17

THE THREE OF THEM ARE LOOKING AT ME WITH THE EXACT same expressions on their faces: confusion.

"So, I don't get it," says Kristy. "You're joining his band?"

"But we're still together, right?" Vlad says. "We're still competing together as the Arden Quartet, right?"

Bas doesn't say anything, but as he looks at me, I sense he might be—disappointed?

"Guys, yes, of course we're still entering this thing together," I say. "I wouldn't just leave you. But Simon says the rules say we can be in more than one band. So I went over to his house yesterday—"

"Simon checked the rules?" Bas sounds like he

doesn't believe me. "And you went to his house?"

I nod at him. "I did. He says he asked Mrs. G. and she said it's okay to be in more than one band. And he has this idea for a sort of rock band and—"

"So you're going to switch to guitar or something?" Kristy sounds confused. And a bit mad.

I don't like how this is going. It's a lot harder than Auntie Flora told me it would be. Last night, after getting home from Simon's, when I went to play tunes for her, she knew something was up.

"Tell me what's what, Flora. You're all a-twitter."

"Oh, Auntie Flora, I don't know. It's just this competition thing. And my friends. And Simon. I don't know what to do."

"Ducky, it's so simple. Just tell your friends the truth." She smiled. "You had fun doing something new and you want to share your talents with *both* bands."

Sure, it sounded so simple when she said it.

But here, on Monday morning, it's not going as smoothly as I had hoped it would.

We're standing at Vlad's locker having this conversation in the hallway before going to homeroom. I had thought about texting them all last night, but…I just couldn't. I thought telling them the truth, face to face, would be better—at least no one could talk behind my back while I waited for them to answer.

"No, I'm not going to switch to guitar." I look around at them. "Guys, we're entering Battle of the Bands as the Arden Quartet, and we're going to play *Final Fantasy*, just like we said. But," I shrug and look around at them, "I'm also going to play my violin in this group that Simon's putting together. Completely different music, different sound."

"Well, I guess if it's in the rules, it's okay," Vlad says. "I just worry about practice time, and any conflicts on the schedule. That kind of thing."

I shake my head. "No conflicts, I promise."

"I thought you weren't interested in a different sound," says Kristy. "You know, like even playing *Final Fantasy* was pushing it. And now—rock music?" She shrugs. "What's going on?"

"I know, I know." It's a good point. "But this is so different. It's not a string quartet. Simon was playing bass guitar, and his dad was doing keyboards and guitars." I shake my head, remembering how very different it was. "It was just so—interesting. I don't know."

I look around at them and hope they understand. Vlad and Kristy are nodding. Bas is just looking.

"I just worry that you'll like that music better and turn into a rocker and start wearing really dark eye makeup and get a tattoo and leave us behind," Kristy says with a super-exaggerated pout that tells me she's trying to be okay with it.

"I promise, no eye makeup."

They all laugh at that and I breathe a huge sigh of relief because I think it's going to be okay.

Bas still hasn't said anything, but when I look at him, he just shrugs and smiles.

"You'll be competing with yourself," he says now. "Which is kind of cool."

"That IS cool!" says Kristy.

"Does your band have a name?" Vlad asks, and then he looks over my shoulder at something behind me. "Oh, hi, Simon."

I turn to see my new bandmate passing by us, on the way to his locker.

"Hi," he says, and nods at us.

I think he just wants to keep walking, but of course, Vlad isn't going to let this opportunity go by.

"Hey, Flora just told us about your band that she joined." Vlad nods, smiling. "It sounds cool."

I don't know how Simon is going to react to this because most of the time he just doesn't react to things—except in music class, of course. But the memory of that first-day turned-down lunch invitation still hangs in the air. Maybe this is Vlad trying a do-over?

Simon's eyes, under his bangs, flick to me and around our group. (Yes, I'm sure Kristy and Bas are watching him, too.) He probably feels outnumbered.

"I was telling them about playing 'Crazy Train' with you and your dad," I come to his rescue. Auntie Flora would be proud of my social skills in this situation. "And how my violin sounded on those rock licks."

"Oh, yeah." He looks around at us again. "Yeah, it was cool."

"Does your band have a name yet?" Vlad, making conversation. And probably curious, too.

Simon looks at me. "Um, no. No name yet."

"That's always the fun part," says Vlad.

"Oh, yeah," says Kristy in a bored voice. "The Arden String Quartet is such a fun name."

"Hey guys! Maybe we should think of something new. For the competition." Vlad is getting into it.

Simon glances at me, a sort of *Nice to see you* glance, and he starts to move off.

"Well, good luck to us all, right?" says Vlad.

"Yeah. Good luck," says Simon.

"Something tells me he didn't mean that," Kristy says in a whisper so only I hear.

"Oh, come on, Kristy. He's just, I don't know, not much of a talker," I say.

"He talks to you okay, apparently," she says. "It's just *us* he doesn't like. This is the *second time* he has basically ignored us."

She nods at Vlad and Bas, who are now listening.

"I'm sure he doesn't dislike you guys," I say, although I'm not quite sure, because apart from conversations about me and my violin, he hasn't exactly shown a lot of friendliness. "He's just, I don't know…"

"Rude? A snob? Stuck-up? Too big and famous for little us?" Kristy is on a roll and it's starting to make my stomach twist.

"Okay, okay," says Vlad, the peacekeeper. "He's okay, Kristy. He just doesn't want to hang out with people. Yet. Right, Flora?"

Vlad to the rescue.

"Right," I say. "That's what I think, too. Let's give him a chance, okay?"

"Fine," says Kristy. "But don't you go turning into a snob, Flora." She gives me a pretend frown when she says it, so I know we're over the worst of this conversation.

"With you keeping me in line?" I pretend to be afraid of her. "Not a chance."

## 𝄞 Chapter 18

"I THINK I SHOULD TAKE HER NOW."

"I think so, too."

My parents are going down the stairs, talking in voices that tell me they don't want anyone to hear.

Strange.

I'm still in a dream. Something about school, and not having homework done, or something. Something worrying.

I roll over and check my phone for the time. 4:06 a.m.

And just like that, I'm awake.

Why are my parents up this early, and who are they talking about "taking" somewhere? Agnes? Auntie Flora?

Agnes is already out of her room and heading for

the stairs when I open my door. We look at each other and I know we're thinking the same thing.

Something is wrong with Auntie Flora.

On Sunday, talking to Simon DeLuca at our kitchen table, and telling me to go have fun playing new music, and then later, when I played tunes for her, she was fine.

But now I remember last night, when I went downstairs with my violin, she was…*off*. Coughing and clearing her throat. Not chatty like usual. Not quick with the comments and jokes about how fast I was playing.

"I'm weary tonight, Ducky," she had said. "I think I'm off to my bed early."

I didn't think anything of it. All I could think of was getting back to my room and finishing up some math homework, and maybe texting with Kristy for a while.

But I'm sure thinking about it now as Agnes and I pause part way down the dark stairs, listening to our parents in the kitchen.

"I'll get her ready," says Mom. "Make sure she has her health card in her purse."

"I'll go warm up the car," says Dad. "Do you need my help persuading her?"

"No. She's really not feeling well. She'll listen to me. Go."

We hear him go out the back door and Mom going downstairs.

"Should we go down?" I ask Agnes.

"I want to know what's happening," she says, but she hesitates.

"I know. She might not want us there if she's not feeling well."

Agnes nods, "What do you think it is?"

I think back to the cough, the weariness. "Maybe a cold?" I shrug. "A bad cold? She was coughing yesterday, remember? And she didn't want me to stay long last night, either."

"She's been going to that exercise session at the Seniors Center," says Agnes. "Who knows what kind of germs are flying around there? And she talks to everyone, of course."

We're sitting on the stairs now, close together. Agnes is wearing her plaid flannel pajama pants and a t-shirt that says *I have no shelf control* with a graphic of a bookshelf. I'm in pajamas with flamingos all over them. I should feel warm, but I don't, and I feel Agnes give a shiver beside me.

Mom and Auntie Flora are coming upstairs from the basement now. The *clump, clump* of their feet, and then their voices.

"It's too much trouble, Sylvia. I can wait until the morning."

"No, lovey. Joe is all ready for you. Warming up the car. It's a good idea to go now. You've got a temperature, and that cough is getting worse. I can hear you breathing."

"I shouldn't have woken you."

"Yes, you should have. I'm glad you did. Here, I've got your coat all ready for you. All right?"

"Just a little shaky." Auntie Flora's voice isn't like her voice. "And this silly cough feeling."

"Hospital," Agnes whispers. "Emergency."

I picture them in the kitchen, getting ready to go out into the dark where Dad has the car warming up.

"I know, I know. It's awful," Mom says. "There. Good to go. Let's get you looked after. They'll know what to do to make you feel better."

"Doctors," says Auntie Flora, sounding a bit more like herself. "I'll probably have to wait hours."

"I'll be there with you," says Mom.

Agnes puts her arm around me. We sit close together and shiver on the dark stairs. I'm sure we're both picturing Mom and Auntie Flora in a too-bright hospital emergency room, waiting for a doctor.

"Let me just leave a note for the girls," Mom says.

We look at each other.

"It's okay, Mom," Agnes calls out. "We hear you."

A moment, and then, Auntie Flora says, "Oh, those two. No secrets in this house." Then, "Go back to your warm beds and I'll tell you all about it later."

Which makes us smile at each other.

"All right, Auntie Flora. If you say so," Agnes calls back.

And I maybe start to feel a bit better, because that sounds exactly like Auntie Flora being herself. But then she coughs, deep and rough, and follows it up with a little sound that might be a wheeze, or a moan.

"Come on, love. Joe's ready," says Mom. "Girls? Go back to bed and I'll check in with you soon, okay?"

"Okay, Mom," says Agnes. "Love you! Feel better, Auntie Flora!"

But I don't say anything, because I can't.

We hear them go out, slow and awkward steps, and then the door closing behind them, and muted voices from the driveway, and car doors closing, and the sound of the car driving away.

"Come on." Agnes still has her arm around me, and we stand up together. "My room."

We snuggle up in her bed and don't talk.

We don't sleep, either. I'm sure we're thinking about the same thing, about Auntie Flora and her cough, and how old she is, and how sick she sounded. How worried Mom and Dad must be to take her to the hospital emergency room this early in the morning.

How one day Auntie Flora is going to leave us.

That's what I'm thinking, and I bet Agnes is, too. But neither of us is going to say it out loud.

## Chapter 19

AGNES AND I DON'T TALK MUCH IN THE MORNING AS WE get ready for school.

"Have some cereal," she says.

She's leaning on the kitchen counter sipping juice, eating toast, and watching me sit at the table with a pencil in my hand, not doing the sudoku. My brain is too fuzzy and full for puzzles this morning.

"Not hungry," I say. It's true. I'm not.

"Eat. You had a bad sleep and you need something to get you through the day." She puts down her juice and opens the cupboard door to get a bowl.

"Okay, Mom." I sit there watching her as she gets out the cereal, the milk, then thumps them down in front of me.

"I'm not hungry either," she says and shrugs.

Her phone buzzes and we both freeze.

"It's Mom." She reads from the screen. *"Saw doctor finally. Moved to a room. Tests ongoing. Probably pneumonia. Auntie doing ok with it all. I'm staying. Dad on his way home now. Get ready for school!"*

We look at each other. Pneumonia. That's bad, isn't it? Especially for Auntie Flora, who is late eighty-something?

"I'm not going anywhere until Dad gets home," I say.

"Me neither. I don't care if I'm late," Agnes says. "Dad can write us a note or something."

I nod and try to eat my cereal. It tastes like wood chips. Not that I've ever eaten wood chips, of course.

When Dad comes in the back door, he looks tired. Morning stubble on his chin, reddish eyes, and his hair looks like he's been running his hands through it. Actually, he looks just like someone who got up early to go wait in a hospital emergency room with a sick aunt.

"I knew you'd still be here," he says. "Come on. I'll call your schools to tell them what's going on and fill you in while I drive you."

It's a short drive to Arden Middle School, so I only get the quick version: nice nurses, fairly quick attention, but then a wait for a doctor and tests, the move to a different room. Auntie Flora sharp as always but definitely not feeling well.

"Don't worry, Flora," he smiles at me as I climb out of the back seat and stand beside the car. "They're looking after her. Mom will let us know."

I check in at the front office, and get a kind smile from Mrs. Botha, who signs me in.

"Your dad called, so you're good to go. Have a nice day, Flora."

The halls are empty and I try to be quiet at my locker. For a moment I just stare at my books piled up and think about turning around and going home. But of course, I don't.

And I really don't feel like going to English class, either, but here I am, coming through the door with the note from the office like a ticket saying it's okay for me to be walking in late.

I know Kristy and Vlad and Bas are looking at me—okay, everyone is looking at me—but I just get busy pulling out my binder and the book we're studying, *The Undercover Book List*, and try not to think about Auntie Flora in the hospital.

Impossible, of course.

"You okay?" Kristy comes up to me at the end of class and we walk out together.

"Yeah. No." Truth.

We walk towards our lockers to change books and get a quick snack before music class. Mommy Agnes put our lunches together while I was upstairs getting ready, so I have no idea what my snack is.

"Everything okay?"

My snack is from Agnes's special stash—dark chocolate rosebuds from that special chocolatier downtown. She knows I love them. Agnes, you're my hero.

"Auntie Flora's in the hospital. Pneumonia, Mom says."

"Oh no! I hope she's okay!" Kristy puts her arms around me for a hug. I hug her back.

Auntie Flora has many little sayings, and one of them is, *It's the kindness that kills you.* I never really thought about what that means, but now I do, because Agnes picking this snack, and that smile from Mrs. Botha, and now Kristy's voice and her hug—it all makes me feel like crying.

I can't speak, so when we pull apart, I just nod and focus on putting books away and reaching for my violin case. (And eating my rosebuds, of course, because everyone knows chocolate is magic.)

It gets better after that. Well, until it gets worse.

"Practice tonight!" Vlad catches up to us as we're walking to music class. He notices my chocolate bar. "Not your usual, Flora, but I like it."

"She needs the extra boost today," Kristy says. "Auntie Flora's in the hospital."

"Oh, no! I hope she's okay," says Vlad.

I take another bite and nod.

"So, practice tonight, right?" Vlad's smart. He knows he should just keep talking and let me and my chocolate bar do our work together. "With Herndorff, and then, I was wondering, can we go back to my house and do some more? On our own?"

He and Kristy talk about this plan and I just listen. "*I have some ideas about the middle part. We'll have to check with Bas, too.*" Whatever they want to do is fine because I'm not even sure I'll be going out tonight. What if there's news from the hospital? What if something happens and I have to stay home...?

Music class is a blur. It's just our string class today, and everyone sounds out of tune to me. *I* sound out of tune to me. The chocolate didn't help me feel more awake, either. So I'm glad when it's finally over and we can pack up and go to lunch. (And I have no idea what my lunch is, either, thanks to Mommy Agnes.)

Kristy and I are just getting to our table where some of our friends are already sitting, when someone says, "Hey, Flora?"

I turn and see Simon standing behind us.

"Oh, hi," I say.

Kristy sits down and pretends not to listen.

"Hi. I was just wondering if you could come over tonight. For a practice, I mean."

Uh-oh.

"I can't tonight. I'm so sorry," I say. And I mean it, because my violin and I would love to go back into that room at the top of his house and figure out what we're going to play for Battle of the Bands. "I already have a rehearsal tonight."

"With her other band," says Kristy, looking up at us.

Simon doesn't react, although I have a feeling Kristy wants him to. He looks at her and then at me. Nods.

"Oh, okay. Maybe tomorrow night?"

"Maybe," I say, wondering what tomorrow is going to look like. Will the news from the hospital be better? Will Auntie Flora be home, maybe? Will she want me to come to her room and play soft, soothing tunes for her? Maybe sing a little "Time is a Fickle Friend"?

But Simon can't read my mind, obviously. He drops his eyes and does a little shake of his head, so his bangs fall down like a screen, and I suddenly realize he thinks I'm avoiding him and his Battle of the Bands plan.

"Okay." And he turns to go.

"But wait," I say quickly. "I really want to, it's just that...it's just a bit complicated right now." I look at him and will him to look back at me. "Auntie Flora's in the hospital, and...I don't know..."

My throat is closing up. Worry and tiredness and the weirdness of standing here having this conversation with Simon DeLuca in front of everyone is catching up to me.

"It's okay," Simon says in a quiet voice, as if he wants only me to hear. "I understand. We'll do it another time. I hope your aunt is okay."

And he nods, reaches out and touches my arm lightly just before he turns and walks away.

# Chapter 20

"IT'S ONLY THREE WEEKS AWAY, GUYS, BUT I THINK YOU'RE in great shape," says Mr. Herndorff. "You've got a great piece there and you sound fantastic."

"Mrs. García told us that there are five entries in our category, and she's seen the list, and it's going to be a real battle," says Vlad. But he doesn't sound scared of battling. He has a grin on his face that I've seen before, such as just before we launch into the most difficult piece in our repertoire. (It's by Bartok. It's a killer.)

"I've seen the list, too," says Mr. Herndorff, nodding. "A classical trio from the Riverside Music School. Other than that, it looks like garage bands trying to bring us into the twenty-first century. No offence, kids." He holds up a hand. "Your choice of 'Lightning's Theme' is inspired, really."

"Did you know Flora is in one of those garage bands?" Kristy can't help herself. "With Simon DeLuca. You know? Theo DeLuca's son?"

Mr. Herndorff leans back and nods, in appreciation, I think.

"Well, that's cool. I heard Theo moved to town. Double duty. It says in the rules that's fine, too. The more the merrier. What's your band's name, Flora?"

Actually, I don't even know. Simon must have picked something and submitted it without telling me.

"No idea," I say.

"Read them out and we'll try to guess." Vlad is super-curious, I can tell. Bas and Kristy nod. I wonder if they're sorry we didn't come up with some fun new name for our quartet. Oh, well. Too late now.

"Okay, let's see." Mr. Herndorff has his computer open and he scrolls a bit until he finds the spot. "Right. Category B, Ages 12-14, here we go. Arden String Quartet, Riverside Trio—okay, that's the other classical group." He nods at us and looks back at the screen. "Right. The other three groups are No Service, Big Kids On The Playground, and Crazy Train." He gets a huge smile on his face. "Oooh, that Ozzy Osbourne track!

Awesome." He looks at me. "Any of those seem possible, Flora?"

Oh, yes. I know exactly what my other band's name is.

"Pretty sure we're Crazy Train." I can't help smiling a little.

And I'll have to thank Simon for choosing it because it's perfect. I will always hear that song and see Simon and his dad and me, up in that music room, playing along to Ozzy. It's where I learned that my violin has another voice. A third voice, if you count the times it transforms into a fiddle playing tunes...

*Auntie Flora...*

"Who else is in your band?" Mr. Herndorff's voice brings me back from my worry place.

"Oh. Simon and me, and I don't know who else."

He nods. "Interesting."

"Maybe you're a duo," says Bas.

"I guess his dad doesn't qualify?" Oh, Vlad. I send him a *You're so funny ha ha* look and he grins at me. "It would be cool, though."

"We haven't talked about it much. I don't even know what we're playing yet," I say, and feel a nervous jolt. The competition is three weeks away and all we've done is jam, once, to Ozzy Osbourne.

"Sounds like you're lucky to be in our band, then,"

says Kristy. "Because we are going to win it all, right, guys?"

It all gets silly then, with the others describing us getting recording contracts and being interviewed by that cool TV show and being invited to perform at The Radio City Music Hall.

"This is our ticket to stardom, guys," says Vlad.

"Hold on, now," says Mr. Herndorff. "I know the pianist from the Riverside group, and she is stellar. And there are some pretty good guitarists that come through our doors here, too. I know one of them was interested in the competition. I think you may be in for a real battle."

"Bring it on," says Kristy, sounding so much like a tough pro wrestler or an action hero that we all laugh.

It feels good to laugh with my friends, and we're still laughing as we wait for our rides home. I said I was too tired for post-practice practice and then Vlad said maybe we could get together on the weekend, instead.

"Text me later, okay?" Kristy says. "I'm going home to do math homework and I know I'm going to need a break. Okay? Promise."

"I will." I know what she's doing: she's not the one who needs a break. "If I'm not asleep."

Yes, sleep would be good, and as I get into the car,

Mom looks at me and obviously comes to the same conclusion.

"You're tired, honey. I hope you don't have much homework, because I'd say from looking at you that you need a big cup of tea, some down time in front of the TV, and bed. Am I right?"

I nod. "Sounds perfect."

And that's what we do, once I finish three questions about integers (interrupted by Kristy, who texted me first). Agnes even comes and joins us. She and Mom and I squish up together on the couch, and Dad tucks us in with the biggest nan blanket we have.

"I remember doing this with two tiny girls about a million years ago," Mom says, and it makes me feel like crying.

The news from the hospital is not bad, but not good. Mom and Dad told us at supper that the doctors think Auntie Flora's breathing is worse, but they're giving her medicine and oxygen and she's a fighter and she even ate something. But it may take a while until she can come home, and much depends on how she responds.

"She's very strong, our aunt," said Dad. "In mind and body."

"And she told me she can't wait to come home and hear some tunes," said Mom. "Although she did suggest having you come to the hospital and play for her there, Flora."

"Really?"

"Sorry, honey, I didn't mean to get your hopes up. I don't think they'd let you do that. You're not even supposed to visit yet." And then she looked at my face, which must have gone into worry mode, and added, "But I love that she's already thinking ahead to coming home."

Mom, trying to be reassuring.

So here we are, curled up together on the couch watching some silly series that Agnes and Mom watch regularly, and I can feel my eyelids drooping and my thoughts spinning away from the TV show.

*Crazy Train. Simon on bass. Me on violin. Someone—who?—on keyboards and singing. I can sing, although I'm better at harmony than lead. I wonder if Simon can sing? I wonder when he was going to tell me the name of our band and who our bandmate is? Bandmates, maybe. Probably tonight, when he wanted to practice. We'll need to practice. Soon. The competition is three weeks away. I should talk to him about Crazy Train at school tomorrow. I should...*

"Crazy Train," I say for no reason and open my eyes.

"Come on, honey," Mom says softly into my ear. "Let's get you to bed."

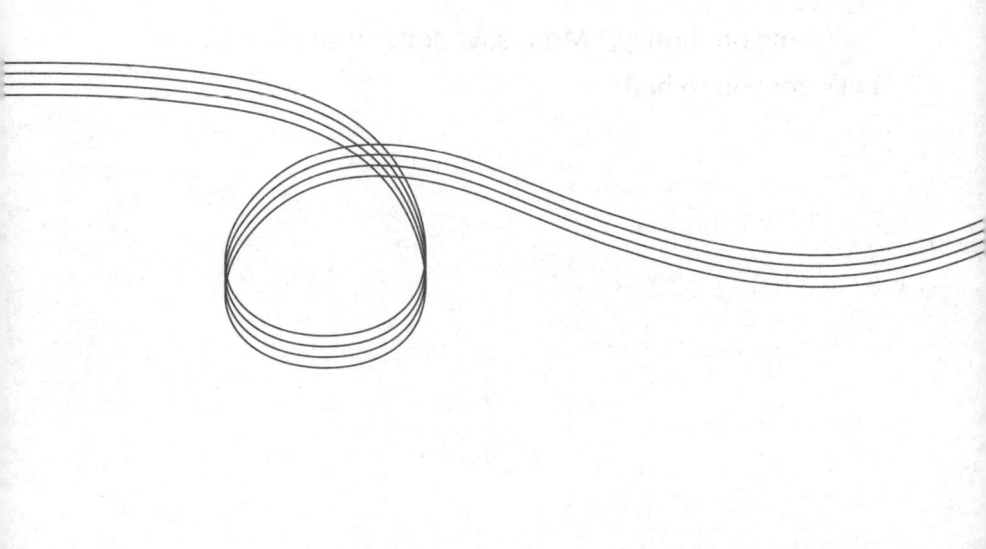

## Chapter 21

SIMON IS AT HIS LOCKER WHEN I GET THERE THE NEXT morning, so I go up to him. I've been thinking about this all the way to school while pretending to listen to Kristy give me a rundown of the same show I watched (slept through?) with Mom and Agnes last night.

"Hey," I say, and he doesn't seem surprised to see me. Maybe he saw me coming.

"Hey."

He doesn't turn to me or anything. I think Kristy would call this "rude behavior," but now that I've seen him in action a few times, I think maybe he's just shy. He keeps taking stuff out of his backpack. Math book. A water bottle. A bag of chips. Goodness, I hope that's not his lunch.

"So, I was at practice at the music center last night, and our teacher named off the bands for the competition, and I was just wondering…"

"What were you wondering?" He tosses his head so his bangs fly off to the side and I can see he's grinning at me, which is a huge change from his usual style. Not rude or shy at all. Kind of out there. It stops me for a moment.

"The name," I say. "Of our band. The band we're entering in the competition."

"Can't you guess? I mean, if you heard all the names, you must know."

I start nodding. He starts nodding.

"Crazy Train. We're Crazy Train, right?"

"I had to come up with something and that seemed good," he says and turns back to his locker to stuff his lunch bag in the bottom. Oh, good. More than chips. "Crazy Train works, right? You're good with that?"

"Yes. That is good. I love it, actually." I don't tell him why I love it—that it captures that moment when I heard something brand new from my violin and how awesome it was. "So, another question."

"Okay." He's finished unpacking now. "Shoot."

"Like, who else is in this band? You're going to play bass, right? And I'm going to do guitar-y stuff on my violin…"

"'Guitar-y stuff'?" He looks at me with an expression that might be *That's funny* but might also be *Are you totally clueless?*

"You know what I mean. But is there a keyboard? Or a singer? A guitarist?" Asking all these questions is making me a bit nervous now, thinking ahead. There's a lot of unknowns here, including what Simon DeLuca is really like, and what strangers I might be hanging out with, and—yikes—what have I gotten myself into? "And what are we going to perform? I mean, what music? And how long will it take me to learn it. I need a bit of time for that. And—"

Simon holds up his hand in a very teacher-like way to stop me talking. It's not rude, but it sure isn't shy, either.

"First, yes, there's another guy in the band. Keenan Delvanian. His dad and my dad work together at the university, but he goes to some independent school here. Maybe you know it, the one with no grades, and lots of free time?"

Ah, yes, I do know that school. We played a concert there once and the kids were wild. The teachers didn't seem to mind, though.

"He's amazing on keyboard, and he can sing really well, too. So that's the first thing. And the second thing, what we're going to play. Keenan and I were thinking 'Don't Stop Believin',' you know, by Journey? It's got some great guitar parts, and everyone likes to sing along when they play it at arenas and stuff. Do you know it?"

I nod. I do know it. Who doesn't know it? Especially if you have a father with an '80s vinyl collection. That guitar-now-violin part, with the really fast runs—okay, that could be interesting. And hard. And interesting.

"So, you good?"

He's looking at me with his head tilted, waiting.

"I'm good." I think that's the right answer. "But we need to practice."

"Well, yeah." He turns back to his locker and pulls out our science textbook from the stack at the bottom. "If you can find the time..."

Wait, is he joking? Or is he actually kind of mad that I didn't agree to practice time last night?

"Um, of course, I—"

He looks at me. "Kidding."

"Oh, good. Good. So—when can we practice?"

"You free tonight?"

I am, actually. I know Dad is planning to visit Auntie Flora after supper. Mom has to go to some meeting at work—something about digitizing county maps or something? Agnes is doing Agnes things, which may mean she's home or not. I'm free to walk the three blocks to Simon's house with my violin.

"Yes."

"See you at 6:30? My house?"

"Okay. 6:30." This is getting real now. I nod and start to move away, back to my own locker where a quick glance tells me Kristy is waiting for me and trying not to watch this little scene. "See you then."

Actually, as I walk away, I realize that more people than just Kristy are trying not to look like they were watching this little scene between Simon and me.

"Don't forget your fiddle," he calls after me, and I'm so frazzled I just wave "okay" and don't even correct him.

# Chapter 22

WE'VE BEEN PLAYING FOR OVER AN HOUR, AND WE SOUND amazing.

No kidding. We sound as good as the original.

Well, maybe not as good as Journey. But I swear we could rock any arena and have people singing and dancing along, waving their phones in the air. It's magical. It's exciting. It's amazing.

It started with me and my violin (or fiddle, not sure now) arriving right at 6:30 and being met at the door by Mrs. DeLuca.

"Oh, you're a brave one, Miss Flora," she said in that gorgeous Southern voice. "Joining up with my little rocker and his pal."

She was smiling though, so I think she was kidding.

"Hi, Mrs. DeLuca. It's okay, really. I'm looking forward to it," I said. "Something new and different, you know?"

"Oh, don't forget, I'm married to an old rocker. I do know all about new and different," she laughed. And then her face changed, and her voice, too. "Simon told me about your auntie, honey." She reached out and touched my arm, just at my elbow, the exact same way Simon did in the hallway the other day. "I'm sending all my best wishes for her to feel better soon."

"Thank you," I said. But I didn't feel like talking about Auntie Flora. In fact, I didn't even want to think about her lying in a hospital bed, sick and scared and not breathing right. Dad went off to the hospital after supper and he promised to hug her for me, but it all just makes me feel worried. So I didn't quite know what to say.

And I think Mrs. DeLuca got that, because she turned on a big smile and pointed to the stairs.

"Up you go," she said. "And I'll come up after a while to see how you're doing. You'll all need some snacks. You're a tea girl, aren't you?" And when I nodded, she nodded back. "Me too, honey. I'll come and rescue you. Go have some fun with those two head bangers."

Simon was right about Keenan. The boy can really play that keyboard.

"Yeah, lessons at Riverside since I was four," he tells me when we take a break and I ask him where he started. "The whole Conservatory thing. The three B's." He means Bach, Beethoven, Brahms—the classics. "Did my Grade Eight last year. They wanted to put me in some Performance stream thing but I don't want to be a concert pianist." He shrugs. "I don't like it when people tell me what to do."

"Wow." That's quite an attitude, I think, but total respect from me. He must be good to get that kind of attention from the pros at the Royal Conservatory of Music.

He nods at my violin.

"You're no slouch," he says. "Heard your quartet at some festival. I don't know, Kiwanis, maybe? Awesome."

"Thanks."

"Okay, okay," Simon interrupts. "You're all great, but back to it. Guys, what do you think about..." and we're off doing some more jamming, fine-tuning entries, deciding where to fit in my "guitar-y" riffs.

From the moment I arrived upstairs, where I could already hear them jamming together—bass and keyboard, and Keenan doing some pretty wild vocals, all of it through amps—we just seemed to be on the same page.

My violin is getting the workout of its life.

"Here," Simon says as he holds out a little clamp with a tiny box on it. "It fits on the side, up near the top bout, so it doesn't get in the way of you bowing. See? It's a pickup. Dad dug it out of his electronics box for us."

I'm playing amplified for the first time ever, using a pick-up that belongs to rock legend Theo DeLuca. I must be in music heaven.

"So cool!" I hand my violin over and watch as he fits the little electronic piece snugly over the wood. "It won't leave a mark, will it?"

"Nope. It's good. See the padding under the clamp? Keeps it from rattling, too. And it'll pick up your strings like crazy." He checks it and moves over the sound board. Adjusts a nob. "Try it."

I draw the bow over the strings and the board lights up. The studio is suddenly full of me.

"I can link it to this distortion box, too," he says, nodding at a black unit sitting on the floor. "Maybe we can add some effects to your violin."

"Is that allowed?"

"I don't know. If not, it should be. I'll check the rules."

I hope it is, because when I launch into the crazy scales-riff thing in our song, I can hardly tell it's a violin. It sounds exactly like an amped-up rock guitar.

In other words, it's magic.

We're having so much fun that we don't even notice how much time has gone by until Simon's mom shows up at the door. She leans there, listening to us until we come to the end, and claps for us.

"Snack time, you three. Come on, it's almost eight o'clock and I'm not sending you home empty."

"We done?" Simon looks around at us, and I realize that I am so done. I'm vibrating with energy from our playing, but I'm also exhausted.

"I think so," I say. "I should probably get home."

"Come and have a cup of tea first, and then we can drive you, or Simon can walk you home," she says. "Come on, kids." She starts back down the stairs.

"Yeah, I should go, too," says Keenan. "I was supposed to be at some school thing tonight. Open house or something."

Wow. I'd be in so much trouble if I blew off a school thing, but Keenan doesn't seem at all worried.

"You should have told me, man," says Simon as we follow him downstairs.

"No worries." Keenan seems very chill about it.

He glances at his phone. "I can still make it if I run. No, thanks, Mrs. DeLuca, I'll pass on snacks," he says as she holds a plate of chocolate chip cookies out toward him. "Well, okay. Maybe just one."

So it ends up being Simon and his mom and me at the table. The tea is hot and strong, just the way I like it. After all the excitement, I'm starting to come down, so tea and cookies at the kitchen table is perfect.

"You three sounded pretty awesome," says Mrs. DeLuca. "I stood part-way up the stairs and listened. My goodness, Flora, you have a way with that fiddle."

"Thank you." And no, I don't tell her it's a violin. Who knows? Maybe I should just start calling it a fiddle all the time, too.

"When's Dad supposed to get home?" Simon asks.

"I guess it depends on how many auditions he has to listen to for his recording class at the university," she says and takes a sip. "Any minute I expect."

I take a glance at my phone and see there's a text from Dad.

"I'm sorry, do you mind if I check this? It's from my dad. He was going to the hospital tonight."

"Of course, honey." Mrs. DeLuca has her mom-face on. "Go on."

The text is to all three of us: Mom, Agnes, and me.

*Going to stay here for a while. Auntie Flora needed the company tonight. Don't worry. She sends her love.*

Right. *Don't worry.*

Don't worry about Auntie Flora, in one of those awful hospital gowns, in a bed, maybe with tubes and machines around her. Nurses coming in and out. Needing company. Feeling sick. Scared, maybe. I bet nobody has brushed her long hair and tied it into that bun she wears. I bet she'd love a cup of Mom's tea. A tune, or a song. Agnes and me singing "Time is a Fickle Friend." Is that why Dad's staying?

Too many thoughts and worries, and they must be all showing on my face as I stare at my phone screen, because Mrs. DeLuca leans across the table and lays her hand on my arm.

"It's going to be okay, Flora, honey. Do you want to go home now?"

*It's the kindness that kills you...*

"Yes, please." My throat feels very tight.

"Simon, you go walk Flora home, please," she says in a voice that tells me she knows how I'm feeling. "It's dark now, and maybe you could both use a little quiet fresh air after all that noisy work upstairs."

She squeezes my arm and lets go, sits back.

"Come on, you two," she says in her usual voice.

"Want to take some cookies to your sister?"

So that's how I find myself walking the three blocks home with Simon DeLuca, in the dark, carrying my violin and a bag of cookies, and having no idea what to say because my head is full of pictures of Auntie Flora in a hospital bed. I wish I were walking home alone.

Simon doesn't speak, either. After about a block, I realize he's not going to start a conversation. Maybe he feels awkward? I mean, there's nothing like having your mom tell you to walk a girl home.

Or maybe he's super-sensitive and knows I don't want to talk? Vlad's like that. Bas, too. The two boys I know the best. Maybe Simon is the same kind of boy. I wonder what my friends would think if they were here right now.

I don't know, but we just walk, and I try to let the rhythm of our footsteps calm me. Deep breaths of cool September air. Our shadows flow in and out of the streetlights.

When we get to my house, I can see Mom's car in the driveway, so that's a relief. She'll want to hear about our rehearsal, which will be a good distraction. She's probably talked to Dad, too, so she'll be able to tell me everything is going to be okay.

But what if it isn't?

"Thanks," I say to Simon. We're at the end of my driveway.

"No problem," he says. "See you tomorrow."

"Yeah. Bye."

"Night."

I turn to walk up the driveway, but turn back when he says, "Hey, Flora?"

"Yes?"

"I hope she's okay."

"Thanks," I say, but he has already turned and is walking away. And I bet he's thinking about his little sister.

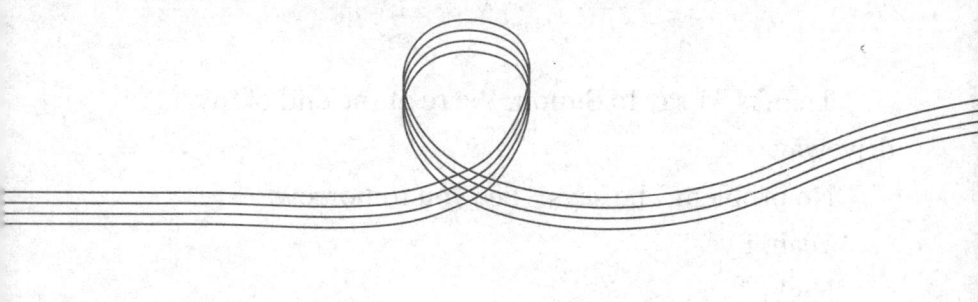

# Chapter 23

"WE SOUND GOOD." VLAD NODS AROUND AT US AFTER finishing our tenth run-through on Saturday morning in his music room.

Yes, Vlad has an actual room in his house completely set aside for music. A grand piano. His cello. A set of five recorders of various sizes all displayed on a stand. And his mother's prized possession (he tells us), an accordion. I've heard her play it and, honestly, she could rival any professional polka player at an Oktoberfest party.

"We sound great!" Kristy wiggles in her chair as if she's just too excited to sit still.

Bas and I look at each other. We *do* sound great.

And that's a good thing because the competition is less than a week away. On Friday night, at the Arden Youth Music Center, we'll be joining all those other bands—yes, like Crazy Train—and playing on the stage in front of judges.

"So, should we run through it again?" Vlad's batteries never run out.

I glance at my phone because a text just buzzed.

"Oh, is that your boyfriend?" Kristy might be teasing, but I'm not sure these days. She means Simon, of course. Crazy Train has been rehearsing a lot over the past two weeks, which means Simon and I are spending a lot of time together.

"He's not my boyfriend," I say. "And no, it's my dad. I have to go now. Sorry, guys."

"No problem," says Vlad. "I hope Auntie Flora's feeling better."

"She is, thanks."

They know what the past couple of weeks have been like for me. Late to some of our rehearsals because I stayed home until Mom or Dad got home with news about Auntie Flora. Trying to fit in time with Crazy Train. A week ago, I had to miss one of our Arden Quartet practices because it was the only time Keenan could meet up for a Crazy Train practice. It's been complicated. And then there's just the constant worry.

Afraid of what the news might be.

"Is she going to die?" I asked Agnes on that really bad night when the hospital called at suppertime and Mom and Dad rushed off without even finishing eating.

Agnes didn't answer right away, which scared me.

"I don't know," she said, finally. We were curled up together under the nan blanket, with the TV light flickering off the walls. "Pneumonia is bad for people Auntie Flora's age. Maybe we should prepare ourselves for bad news."

I looked at her and saw a tear sliding down her cheek. I think that scared me more than anything.

"I'm going to hope for good news," I said, and Agnes hugged me.

"Good idea. Me too."

Then it was good news, finally. Mom said that Auntie Flora just made up her mind, that she was fed up with being sick and she was going to get better and come home. Apparently, she said: "They don't know how to make a decent pot of tea here, Sylvia. I ask you. Is that so hard?"

"That's when I knew," said Mom. "The worst was over."

"When Auntie Flora starts complaining about the tea, look out," said Dad.

That was a week ago. It's such a relief to be able to say, finally, that Auntie Flora is out of the hospital. She's not home yet, though. She's at a sort of rest place, a convalescent home, Mom says. And I'm finally going to get to visit her. Today.

I pack up my violin and music folder and stand up to go.

"So, Tuesday night with Herndorff?"

"Yup, that will be our last tune-up. Or do we want to practice once more on Wednesday night?" asks Vlad. "But honestly, I think we could play now and win the whole thing." He grins at me. "Might even beat Crazy Train."

"I think we have to watch out for Big Kids On The Playground," says Bas. "I heard Pierre and Rudy practicing, and they are really rocking out."

"I'm not worried," says Kristy. "We're different, right? Cool new-age music in a classical setting."

"You just got the job of publicist," says Vlad, pointing at her, and she laughs, because she would make an excellent publicist and we all know it.

"Um, I don't know about Wednesday, guys," I say.

"Oh?" Vlad scrunches up his face, surprised.

Bas looks over at me with an expression I can't quite place. Disappointed?

Kristy doesn't hold back, though.

"Simon DeLuca wins again, right?" she says.

"Kristy, come on." Wow. The way she says it stings a bit. "You guys know I'm in two bands. It's hard to juggle."

"Or you could just choose," says Kristy. "I mean, come on, Flora. I know Auntie Flora is sick and that's been hard, but sometimes I think you just blow off our practices so you can spend time with the cool new boy."

There's a horrible silence as I process what she just said. She's mad at me for spending time with Simon. For being in Crazy Train and trying something new.

"Come on, Kristy," says Vlad, the one who always smooths things over. "It hasn't been that bad."

"Okay, I know," Kristy says and sighs. She looks at me then. "But it hasn't been the same. Yes, I know you're worried about Auntie Flora, but wow, you're really spending a lot of time with that jerk. And what happened to only wanting to play classical stuff? Remember that, at the beginning? We practically had to drag you kicking and screaming into this *Final Fantasy* piece."

I look at her, stunned. Is that what happened? I look

over at Vlad, and he just shrugs. He must agree with her about Simon, and me, and the music.

"The cool new boy," says Bas. I look at him, confused, and he shrugs. "Just repeating what she said. He's also a jerk, I guess."

"He's not a jerk," I say. I can't believe I have to defend Simon DeLuca to my friends. I can't believe I'm using this mad voice, either. I never talk to them this way.

But Kristy never talks to me this way, either.

"I don't know what you're so worried about," I say. My voice doesn't even sound like my voice. "You've been calling him a jerk and a snob but you don't even know him."

"Well maybe that's because he can't be bothered getting to know *us*." Kristy's voice matches her face. She's mad. "Too rich for us. Famous daddy. Can play any instrument. Cool long hair. Whatever. He's got you sucked into his special little world and now you don't even have time for a rehearsal. It's like you don't even want us to win this thing."

I'm so stunned I don't even know what to say.

"Come on, now, Kristy," says Vlad, stepping in. "It's not that bad." He looks at me and shrugs. "But…you do seem kind of overbooked, though."

"Overbooked?" My voice goes up an octave. "I was doing *fine*, but then Auntie Flora..." Oh, no! I'm going to start crying! "I have to go," I say without looking at them.

"Flora! Wait!" Vlad calls after me, but I ignore him.

Dad's waiting in the car outside Vlad's house, a big smile on his face. I try to smile back as I climb in with my violin.

"She'll be so happy to see you, too," Dad says. "When Agnes visited last night, Mom said she could see her improving by the minute." He smiles over at me. "You girls are part of the cure, you know."

I just smile and don't say anything because I'm still rattled from that conversation (or, was it a fight?) with my friends. Also, to tell the truth, I'm a bit worried about what I'm going to see. Will Auntie Flora look different?

"You'll have so much to tell her. About school, and the competition. She'll want to know how your two bands are doing." Dad glances at me. "She was asking about the DeLucas. She really enjoyed meeting them at the fire that night."

Well, I'm going to have to think about what to tell her about the competition and how my two bands are doing, because right now I'm not really sure. Also, I wonder what she was asking about the DeLucas?

"And I know she'd love to hear some tunes," Dad says, bringing me back from that dark firepit to our car on a sunny Saturday morning. "Maybe you could bring your fiddle in, and we'll see if it's okay?"

"Can we?"

"Let's give it a try. She'd love it."

*She'd* love it? I think I'd love it more. I realize suddenly that I haven't played any tunes the whole time she's been away. It's as if my fingers went on strike.

Okay, yes, there have been rehearsals with the quartet and with Crazy Train, so it's not like I haven't been playing.

But playing tunes, especially playing tunes for her...

A song comes on the car radio and Dad starts to sing along. The sun is so bright I have to flip down the car visor. I'm holding my fiddle case—it's not a violin case right now—between my knees, and I imagine the instrument vibrating with excitement: *Tunes? I get to play some tunes again, finally?*

Of course, instruments can't think. But I can. Sometimes I think too much, and right now my head is full of Kristy's words and the idea that my friends don't like Simon and don't understand why I'm playing in a band with him. What Kristy said about our choice of music, and how I wanted us to keep our music classical and familiar, and then I go diving into rock violin riffs with new boy Simon.

I'm confused and rattled and, okay, yes, my feelings are hurt.

Tunes are exactly what I need right now.

## Chapter 24

DAD ASKS THE NURSE AT THE FRONT DESK IF IT'S OKAY FOR me to play my fiddle in Auntie Flora's room.

"Oh, that would be lovely," he says. "I bet some of the other residents will be listening in." He smiles at me. "You might attract an audience, just saying."

His nametag says "Alek," and I think I smile back, but I'm not sure, because I'm suddenly really nervous about walking into Auntie Flora's room and seeing her. I don't want her to look different. I don't know what I'll do if she's thinner, or frailer, or looks unhappy.

"Oh, don't worry," says Alek. He obviously thinks the weird look on my face is because I'm afraid of playing in front of an audience. "People here love a distraction. They'll be your fans. Applause, dancing, the works. Prepare yourself."

Okay, the scene he's describing makes me smile a little but I know the Wellington Convalescent Home is full of elderly people recovering from illnesses and surgery. Something tells me dancing isn't included in the doctor's prescription.

"Great, thanks, Alek," says Dad. "We'll tell you how it goes."

"Oh," Alek shakes his head, grinning. "You won't need to. I'll hear all about it, don't you worry."

I feel Dad's arm around my shoulders as we walk down the corridor towards the hallway where Auntie Flora's room is.

"It'll be fine, Ducky," he says. "She told me she can hardly wait to see you."

The hallway is full of doors, some of them open. I try not to look in rooms as we pass by, but it's hard not to. Some residents are sitting in chairs by bright windows. I hear TVs broadcasting the baseball game. Snippets of conversation.

We pass a room where a woman is speaking in Punjabi, sounding like Bas's mother. Fast and light, ending with a laugh. Someone laughs back.

"Here we are," says Dad.

Now. I take a deep breath just before going through the door and—

There she is. Sitting as upright as ever in a comfy chair by the window, wearing her favorite blue cardigan and her stretchy pants. She—or someone—has done her hair into that bun she likes. She looks exactly the same. And she's smiling.

"Ducky! My Flora!"

She pushes herself out of her chair and stands there with her arms out toward me, so of course the fiddle gets tossed on the bed and I run over for a hug and squeeze my eyes shut to stop the little bit of tears starting. But it's just because I'm so, so, so happy to see her.

"And you've brought your fiddle," she says into the top of my head as we rock back and forth in the best hug ever. "I've been missing our tunes."

So I get out my fiddle, tune it up, and play tunes. And yes, Alek was right. We do attract an audience.

"We have a big week this week," says Auntie Flora to me after my little tune concert, when things have quietened down and Dad has gone to check at the front desk about the discharge procedure this week.

It's just the two of us. Auntie Flora in her chair, me on the bed.

"It will be so nice to have you home," I say. "You're going to love your new room. It's smaller, but the view into the backyard is way nicer than what you had down in the basement."

We've been busy converting my mother's sewing room on the main floor into a bedroom for Auntie Flora, so that she doesn't have to go downstairs.

"I so rarely use it for sewing these days," Mom had said.

She was right, too. It's the place where we stored stuff when we didn't know where else to put it. So all four of us have been sorting piles of books, clothes, winter coats, and big packages of paper towel and tissues that Dad buys in bulk. Now we can actually see the bed, freshly made up with Auntie Flora's favorite quilt. The sewing machine is gone, along with the little cabinet of supplies, and there's now a dresser, with the TV on top, ready for her romcoms or the nightly news. And the bathroom is right there, too, just outside the door.

Not to mention it's only steps from the kitchen—and the tea pot.

"Oh I have all the view I want, right now, Ducky," she says, smiling at me.

I don't know why, but I feel my eyes filling up with tears.

She reaches out for my hands and holds them.

"It was a bad time," she says, and nods at me. "But things are getting better. I'm feeling better. And what fun we have ahead of us. Life is good right now, Ducky. And you have your music contest this week, and I'll be able to hear you play with your friends and your new friend. That nice boy."

Hmmm. Not sure "nice boy" is the description most people would use for Simon DeLuca, but Auntie Flora is definitely not most people.

She sees things other people don't always see. Like right now. She sees me and knows—well, I think she knows all the things I've been worrying about. Worrying about her being sick and maybe never coming home. Worrying about Battle of the Bands, and trying to make all my friends, old and new, happy. She sees Simon the way I wish everyone would see him, as a boy who is dealing with things.

"Well, we should be off," says Dad, coming into the room. "Sylvia will be in tomorrow to visit. And Tuesday is home day." He beams at us both, "Isn't that great?"

"It certainly is," says Auntie Flora, still looking at me. "It is the greatest."

And she squeezes my hands and lets go, nodding at me to make sure I agree.

"Oh, Flora put on quite a show," Dad says at supper that night.

"Oh, my goodness, I hope you didn't get in trouble with the management," says Mom.

"No, no, it was great." Dad laughs. "A guy with a walker and an oxygen tank stopped by the door. Did a few jig steps and had to stop."

"Ernie," I say. "From Montreal."

"Right, right." Dad nods. "And that other lady, Estelle? The one with the daughter-in-law?"

"They stood at the door and told us Estelle was going home tomorrow and this was the best goodbye party ever." I lean over to serve myself more macaroni from the big casserole dish Mom put in the middle of the table because I'm famished. I think I'm eating more tonight than I have for weeks. "She said Auntie Flora has been a wonderful neighbor."

"Goodness, it sounds just like a little village over there in the Wellington," Mom laughs.

"Well, you always know Auntie Flora is going to get

the party started, right?" says Agnes. "When I was there on Thursday, two ladies stopped by and asked if she was coming to the exercise class later and Auntie Flora said she wouldn't miss it but she hoped they included some music and dancing this time."

Of course she did. We all laugh and it feels so good.

"You should have heard Flora," says Dad. "She was great. Played the whole Newfoundland tune repertoire. The place was rocking."

"Oh, Dad," I say as they all laugh at me. "It was not!"

He's right, though. I ran through all her favorites—"Mussels in the Corner," "Cyril Foote's Tune," "Pretty Little Mary," "Cuckoo's Nest," "Coming From the Races"—and she was so happy, clapping along. And I only heard her cough once.

"And she's coming home this week," Dad says, which is the best part of all.

## Chapter 25

VLAD TEXTS ME ON SUNDAY NIGHT: *THINGS GOT WEIRD there yesterday. You ok?*

Vlad. The peacekeeper. I can always count him to at least try to make me feel better.

*I'm ok. Sorry for leaving so quick.*

*How is your aunt?*

*Great! Coming home this week. Played some tunes for her.*

He sends a *YAY* complete with a celebration emoji that incudes a champagne bottle and fireworks and follows it up with: *The healing power of music!*

Hmmm. I wonder if music can heal the tension I feel from Kristy. Maybe I should ask Vlad what he thinks about that? But he's already a step ahead of me, as usual.

*Don't mind Kristy. We're not used to sharing you!*

Maybe. I think it's more about who they're sharing me with.

Auntie Flora calls him a "nice boy," but I know Kristy and the kids at school think Simon's not very friendly. He doesn't try to join in. Does he think we won't like him? Does he think he's different, or maybe better than us? It's only because Rudy was so chill that he was able to get his choice of percussion, and we all watched *that* drama unfold. Not going for lunch with Vlad that first day. People remember stuff like that. I remember stuff like that.

But I've also seen him sitting at my kitchen table talking to Auntie Flora. I've jammed with him and had an amazing time making music. His mom hugged him that night I was at his house, and he hugged her back. I've seen a different boy.

And then there's the whole little sister thing, but I try not to think about that.

Vlad interrupts my thoughts: *See you tomorrow. Big week!*

*See you tomorrow.*

Later, just as I'm getting ready for bed, I get a text from Kristy.

*Yay Auntie Flora coming home. See you tomorrow!* And a heart emoji.

I heart emoji right back at her—and silently thank Vlad for doing such a great job at peacekeeping.

♪

"Things are going to be calm and normal," I tell myself as I wait for Kristy at the corner on Monday morning.

And it turns out, I'm right. Whatever happened during that, um, *conversation* at Vlad's seems to have disappeared from her memory.

Either that, or she's making a really big effort, probably because Vlad told her to.

"Hey! Great news about Auntie Flora," she said when she walked up. "And wait until I tell you about the movie we went to yesterday."

We walk to school together without even mentioning those awkward moments at Saturday's rehearsal. Yup. Calm and normal.

But in fact, it's not a very calm and normal week.

First, our principal, Mr. Andrechuk, gets the ball rolling on Monday morning.

"So be sure to come out and cheer the Boys' soccer

team this afternoon, and the Girls' soccer team on Tuesday as they both face off against Maryhill right here on our field."

Kristy and I exchange a quick look and a tiny head shake, and it feels just like normal. *Sorry, Mr. Andrechuk, we'll be busy rehearsing on Tuesday after school.* It's as if he sees us, though, because then he continues.

"And remember, everyone, the Arden Youth Music Center's Battle of the Bands competition is this Friday night at the AYMC auditorium on Main Street, and we have several entries from Arden Middle School, including the Arden String Quartet, featuring Vladimir Bachman, Kristy Carpenter, Bas Malik, and Flora Parsons. And then we have..." there's a pause where he's obviously checking his notes. "Big Kids on the Playground, featuring Rudy St. Louis, Pierre Martin, Sol Silver, Arnav Shah, and Francis DiLello."

"Power rock right there," says Vlad out loud and everyone laughs, including Sol and Arnav, who are in our homeroom.

"...and also from AMS is Flora Parsons, again, and Simon DeLuca, who are Crazy Train."

Everyone glances back at Simon but he doesn't look up. He just keeps doodling on the back of a notebook, head down, bangs covering his eyes.

I don't look at Kristy because I have a pretty good idea of what she's thinking right now—and I think it would best to avoid going there.

"And there are a couple of other bands, from other schools in the area. So please, go out and support your classmates on Friday night. It is a fundraiser for the Center, so ticket sales will help. Donations too, and yes, an email has been sent to families, so the word is out. Now, my last announcement is about the Grade Six trip to the museum next week..."

Yes, the word is out. Melina comes up to ask me about it at the end of class.

"Maybe next year I'll try to enter," she says in her shy way.

"You should! You and Brenda. Remember? Vlad suggested that. Her flute and your zheng really would be awesome together," I say. Melina's so shy, but I've seen her perform in front of the school before, and she seems to disappear into her playing. "I'm going to remind you."

"Okay!" and she laughs with me.

Vlad and Bas sit with Sol, Rudy, and Arnav at lunch and I'm pretty sure they're trash talking each other's bands. In the most fun way possible, of course, because Vlad would never go darkside.

♪

On Tuesday I get a text from Mom at lunch: *SHE'S HOME!!!*

She sends a photo of Auntie Flora sitting at the kitchen table with a cup of tea and a huge smile. I almost cry.

"Let's see," says Kristy, who's sitting across from me. "Awwww. Auntie Flora!"

Supper is all laughter and Lightning Round. Auntie Flora wins, of course.

"As I was leaving St. Joseph's today, Nurse Alek came over and gave me a little hug and told me I was his favorite and it was going to be very dull without me," she says. "I told him life was going to be very dull without him, too, and he actually blushed."

"Oh, Auntie Flora," says Agnes. "What a flirt!"

Auntie Flora just shrugs and sips her tea. "Me? Never."

We all laugh, of course, and it feels so good. I wish I could stay here at the kitchen table with them all, but it's our quartet's last rehearsal tonight.

"Off you go," she says as I stand up from the table to get ready. "I'll be here when you get home. And if I'm still awake," she cracks her head to one side and gives me a quick wink.

I know exactly what she means. *Tunes.*

Later, when we finish our last run-through, Mr. Herndorff just shakes his head—with a big smile on his face, of course.

"You guys. If you don't win this on musical performance alone, I don't know what the judges are thinking. Your execution is flawless. And the emotion you convey with those instruments—so, so good." He shakes his head the way you do when you don't know what words to use. But he's not done, yet.

"And hey, it's true, they might be looking for something different, you know? The whole rock band thing? Who needs classical music and old-school instruments anymore?" We know exactly what he's talking about: Crazy Train. No one looks at me, though. "Doesn't matter. I'm so proud of what you guys have done with this piece. You're winners in my book."

Of course, he has to say that. He's our teacher, after all. (But we all love hearing it from him, just the same.)

"And remember, it is a competition," he goes on. "Which means there will be a table of judges sitting there watching you. And I just read that the panel includes our *favorite* judge from Kiwanis, remember him? The music professor, Dr. Ennis-Holt."

Mr. Herndorff's former professor in the music program. Short, a big bushy beard, and eyebrows that practically covered his eyes. An English accent that made everything sound serious (or hilarious, according to Vlad, who watches a lot of British comedies). He still gave us a gold medal at Kiwanis last year, but he was scary. Especially when he came up to us afterward to have a short conversation with Mr. Herndorff.

"Teaching, Lawrence? I truly thought you had a performance career ahead of you."

"Teaching, Dr. Ennis-Holt," said Mr. Herndorff. "And loving every minute of it." He turned to us. "Especially with students like these."

"Hmmm. Yes. Talented group."

He nodded at us and walked off, and Mr. Herndorff called him a bad word under his breath that we all pretended we hadn't heard.

Oh, yes, we all remember that guy.

"Oh, great," says Vlad. "Well, we'll just have to wow him, right?"

"Stare him down," says Kristy.

"Play the way we play," says Bas, and we all nod at each other. Our team. Together, win or lose or whatever happens.

And then on Wednesday morning:

"Tonight?" Simon says to me in the hallway before homeroom.

"Okay," I say, and watch him walk away towards our classroom, alone.

## Chapter 26

MY EYES ARE CLOSED AND I'M SO WRAPPED UP IN THE sound we're making—Keenan's voice and his amazing keyboard playing, Simon's bass doing not just notes but rhythm, and my violin running up and down the scales and sounding just like a wailing rock guitar—that I don't even notice Simon's dad is now leaning on the door frame, hands in the pockets of his faded jeans, listening to us with his eyes closed.

It's only when we come to the end, with Keenan's voice hanging on to those last words while Simon and I fade out, that I come back to the real world.

"Sounds great, guys," says rock legend Theo DeLuca.

I think Simon and Keenan must be as dazed as I am

by our playing because none of us replies right away. Then Simon seems to wake up.

"Hey. Thanks, Dad. Were you there the whole time?"

"Nah. Stood on the stairs for a while. Just came up for the last bit." He nods at Keenan. "Great fade on the voice there at the end. Works great with the fiddle."

Then he looks at me and I get the nod, too. Or at least, my fiddle does. "Awesome. Any band I know would love to have that kind of wailing stuff going on."

"Thanks," I say. I might be blushing because I just got a really cool compliment from a famous rock star.

"Amazing how a fiddle can capture the voice of a guitar." He's still nodding at my fiddle, but then he looks at me and smiles. "You've got rock genes in there somewhere."

Wow. The famous rock star is still saying nice things about me. Wait until I tell Dad. He'll love this.

"So, do you think we're ready?" Simon says. "For Friday?"

"You're ready," says his dad. He has a very sleepy looking face. Droopy eyes and not a lot of expression. Gray hair that's floppy, like Simon's. Leaning there in the doorway in old jeans and a plaid shirt over a gray t-shirt, he could be anybody. "Looking forward to seeing you perform."

"So we have to be there at six, right?" Keenan asks as he stands up from the keyboard. "Are we done here for tonight?"

Keenan is always the first to leave our rehearsals. I have a feeling he's one of those people who leaves all his schoolwork until last thing at night.

"Yeah, I guess," says Simon, which makes me think he probably wanted to run through things again.

"Great, okay." Keenan pulls on his hoodie and grabs his pack. "See you guys at the place on Friday night then. Later."

Mr. DeLuca has to step in a bit to let Keenan by and they exchange a nod.

"You should probably see him out," he nods at Simon, who gives a sort of grunt, peels off his bass guitar and sets it in the stand.

"I'll be right back," he says to me.

"Okay."

So, here I am, standing awkwardly in Mr. DeLuca's office, or recording studio, or whatever it is, with him leaning in the doorway, looking at me and my fiddle.

I'm not sure what comes next. Should I talk to him, maybe? Ask a question?

Turns out I don't have to do a thing.

"Feel like playing some tunes?"

What? Really?

"Um, sure."

He heads over to the keyboard and hits a few chords, going up the keyboard chromatically. Impressive. But, of course, we're talking about Theo DeLuca here, so why am I even surprised he can effortlessly play chords in all keys up and down the keyboard?

"So," he says, "Whatcha got?"

*Focus, Flora! The rock legend wants some tunes!*

"I could play some of the tunes my aunt likes, from Newfoundland? Is that okay?"

"Is that okay?" He smiles at me then, and it cracks his face open and changes him completely. "That's perfect. Lead on."

So of course I start with "Jim Rumbolt's Tune." I forget to tell him what key it's in, but it doesn't matter. He's right there. Rhythm, notes, left hand solid on bass notes, right hand jumping on the chords and adding little bits of ornamentation.

We play it three times through and then I switch to "Father's Jig," and he follows the key change no problem, even without me giving the "hup" that the fiddler is supposed to give to let everyone know you're changing tunes.

Now we are rocking. Auntie Flora would not approve

of the tempo I'm setting, but Mr. DeLuca doesn't seem to mind.

The sound of clapping.

I turn towards the door, still playing, and there's Simon and his mom, and she's clapping along.

"Oh! I love this!" she calls out to us. "Simon, honey, go get the drum. You know, the drum?"

Simon goes over to one of the cabinets, reaches around for a few seconds and comes up with a round hand drum. A bodhran. Simon knows how to play a bodhran? I only know about them because on a trip a few years ago, Samuel Parsons (third cousin twice removed, or something) played his at a kitchen party in someone's house.

"Only one bodhran allowed at a session," one of the uncles said then. "Two bodhrans is death to the tunes."

I have no idea what that meant then, but right now, I realize that Simon DeLuca definitely knows how to play the bodhran, and he's on his own, so it's perfect.

We are rocking these tunes. So many thoughts are spinning through my head right now, alongside the notes, and one of them is, *Where did Simon DeLuca learn to play bodhran?* Doesn't matter.

His playing adds that crazy rhythmic *thrum*, sometimes steady, sometimes syncopated. He's so good at it.

"Hup!" I yell. "Switching to D!"

And we're into "Kitty's Rambles."

"I could dance right now!" yells Mrs. DeLuca from the doorway.

"You go right ahead, honey," Mr. DeLuca calls from the keyboard, so she does.

She steps and stomps—I think it's called "clogging"—around the room as we play. I can't help grinning as I dance my bow over the strings, and when I look at Simon and his dad, they're both grinning, too. Watching her.

Watching her dance. So happy. This room is completely full of *happy* right now.

But it's the third tune, and most sets end on three tunes, so I dip my fiddle and change the last B part a bit. Of course, Simon and his dad totally get the cue, and we wrap it up in a big three beat finale. Drum, keyboard, and fiddle, together.

"Nice playing," Mr. DeLuca says to me. "Great set, there."

"Oh, I just loved it!" Mrs. DeLuca comes over and gives me a hug. "I wish your auntie could have been here for this."

"Me too," I say, and mean it from the bottom of my heart.

"And Simon, honey, you had that beat nailed," she goes and gives him a hug, too. "Now, come on, you three. I've got a snack ready downstairs. Let's go. You're done for the night."

A snack sounds good to me, and yes, I am definitely done for the night.

"Thank you," I say. "And then, I think I need to be going. It's getting late."

"Of course, honey. Do you want a ride? Or Simon can walk you again?"

"My dad said he'd get me tonight, but thanks."

I loosen my bow and start packing my fiddle away in its case. It's just Simon and me now, and we can hear his mom still talking as they go downstairs.

"Thanks for doing that," he says. "We never know when Dad's going to want to play something, and it's great that you were here. Something different."

"I loved it," I say. "I don't get to play tunes with other people. It's always just me playing for Auntie Flora. So this was really cool. Your dad is so good. Like, I didn't even need to tell him the keys or anything. It's like he totally knew the tunes already."

Simon closes the cabinet door and stands up. He puts his hands in his jeans pockets and shrugs. Actually, he suddenly looks a lot like his father.

"He knows everything about music. I mean everything. He's a genius, but since Grace died, he just doesn't play much."

We look at each other across the room. There are so many things I want to say—know I should say—but I'm frozen.

He shrugs again.

"Come on. Let's go get a snack," he says, and leads the way past me towards the stairs. "I think Mom made pie."

So I just follow him.

# 🎼 Chapter 27

IT'S THURSDAY NIGHT AND I'M IN MY ROOM DOING HOMEwork—well, I'm supposed to be doing homework, but mostly I'm staring into space thinking about all the big things filling my head right now.

Like, Battle of the Bands, and the Arden String Quartet versus Crazy Train, and how the Arden String Quartet didn't rehearse last night and that's fine with me.

Famous rock star Theo DeLuca playing tunes last night. Playing tunes with ME.

*...but since Grace died...*

Battle of the Bands. Again.

*...but since Grace died....* Again.

I rub my hands over my face and groan. It's awful when unwanted thoughts and images crowd into your head without warning and you can't do anything to stop them or slow them down.

And now I can't help thinking that must be exactly what it's like for Simon and his parents. That car accident. They must see it over and over and over. And hear it. And feel it.

*...but since Grace died...*

So when the doorbell rings and I hear Mom go to answer it, I lean back in my chair and welcome the distraction.

"Well, hello!" I can tell from Mom's voice that the person she's saying hello to is someone unexpected.

"I hope you don't mind, Sylvia."

That Southern drawl is unmistakable. Why is Simon's mother at our door? Of course, I get up out of my chair and stand by the door so I can hear better.

"We had such a lovely visit with your sweet Flora last night," Mrs. DeLuca is saying. "And she told us Auntie Flora was home, and I just wanted to bring her this. A sort of 'get well' and 'welcome home' present."

"Oh, Petra! How kind of you! Come in, come in."

"Oh, I don't want to intrude, if you're busy or if she's sleeping, or anything."

"Don't be silly. Come on. She'll be delighted to see you. I'll put the kettle on." A pause, and then Mom says in that *Moms-hanging-out-together* voice, "Unless you'd like a glass of wine?"

"Oh, tea will be just fine with me," says Petra, and they laugh together.

Oh, wow. Look at Mom hanging with her new friend.

Agnes sticks her head out of her bedroom door and we exchange a look. I'm pretty sure she's thinking the same thing I am. *Moms!*

"Girls!" Mom calls up the stairs. "Break time! We have a visitor!"

Agnes and I do not need any more encouragement to leave our homework behind. Down the stairs we go.

"Well, isn't this fun," says Auntie Flora as she joins us a few minutes later. "We're having a kitchen party."

"I wanted to bring you this," says Mrs. DeLuca, and she lifts something out of the big bag she has beside her. "Nothing much, but my mama taught me it was nice to let people know when you're happy for them. And I'm very happy you're feeling better and are back home with your lovely family."

It's a huge pie with a golden-brown crust laced across the top, and baked apples seeping through.

"Oh my!" Auntie Flora's eyes go wide. She reaches out for Mrs. DeLuca's hands across the table. "Thank you, so much, my dear. This is such a treat. You are so kind."

"Flora was just telling us about the piece of pie she had last night after practice," says Mom. She's already assembling plates and cutlery. "She raved about it. We are in for a treat. You get the first piece, though, Auntie Flora."

Agnes is at the counter keeping an eye on the kettle and I'm taking mugs down from the cupboard. We are a well-oiled Tea and Pie Kitchen Party Machine here at the Parsons house.

"Well, I don't mind," says Auntie Flora.

It's a girl's night all right. Dad's working late, so it's just us Parsons girls. And Mrs. DeLuca, who fits right in.

Tea is poured. Pie is served. Conversation starts with Auntie Flora's time at the Wellington, her return home to her new little room here on the main floor, and how convenient it is for the kitchen.

"Although, I have no problem doing stairs," she says, and doesn't see Mom, Agnes, and me exchange a look. We heard her wheezing on the stairs when she went down to retrieve something yesterday.

"Well, that's just perfect. It's always important to be near the tea pot," says Mrs. DeLuca. Oh, yes. She totally fits in with us Parsons.

And then she turns to Agnes and asks about school. Of course, Mom jumps in and brags about how Agnes just won some school scholarship prize that means she can attend a science conference thing in November, and that will probably help with her university applications.

"What amazing girls you have, Sylvia," says Mrs. DeLuca. "This brainiac here," she nods at Agnes. "And, of course, this little musical prodigy." She reaches out and rests her hand on my arm. "We had such a lovely time last night, did she tell you? She played some of your Newfoundland tunes, Auntie Flora, and I even got to clog a little. Reminded me of my youth at the Charlotte County Fair."

"Your clogging was very cool," I say.

"Well, thank you! Couldn't help dancing to those wonderful tunes. And both my boys even joined in with the music. It was so fun." She stops and her face changes a little. Her smile slips.

"Both my boys," she says again. She's smiling at Auntie Flora but I'm sure she's thinking about what Simon told me, how his dad doesn't play much anymore. And why.

Mom, Agnes, and Auntie Flora are quiet, watching her. Last night I told them about more than just the pie. I told them what Simon said after his dad played the keyboard and had so much fun. What he said before we went back downstairs.

We all know we're looking at someone who lost a child, and maybe a bit of her husband as well, in that accident.

Awkward. There's a moment's silence, and then Auntie Flora says, "You know, Petra, I lost a son."

Agnes and I glance at each other. Is this really the best time to talk about our distant cousin Joe Parsons, the fisherman, lost during a gale, when he was just eighteen? Apparently, it is.

"Did you?" Mrs. DeLuca goes very still. She looks at Auntie Flora. "I'm so sorry."

"We still talk about Joe, though. About his silly jokes, and how he never wanted to cut his hair. And how much our Joe here," she nods at Agnes and me, "the girls' dad, looks just like him."

Mrs. DeLuca is frozen, watching Auntie Flora.

"I heard that you lost a child," Auntie Flora continues. "I'm so very, very sorry."

Agnes and I glance at each other in horror. What is Auntie Flora *doing*? Mrs. DeLuca comes with a pie for a friendly visit and suddenly she's at a table with a bunch of strangers, basically, having someone talk about—well, about something awful. Something private.

Mom is quiet and still, and I take a quick glance at her, too. But she's just watching Auntie Flora. She's not worried like Agnes and me. Okay, maybe this is fine. Maybe this is what adults do?

"Yes," says Mrs. DeLuca, still watching Auntie Flora. "I had a daughter. Grace. There was a car accident. It was all over the news, which was awful. Nobody's fault, but Theo was driving." She looks down then. Maybe trying to get pictures out of her head.

"I'm so terribly sorry," says Auntie Flora. "Grace. What a lovely name. What was she like?"

Mrs. DeLuca looks up again, and there's a moment when I hold my breath, thinking, *She's going to stand up and walk out.*

But that's not what happens. Mrs. DeLuca smiles. Okay, a sort of sad smile, but still a smile.

"She was a little madam. She had us wrapped around her baby finger. Especially her daddy. She could read by the time she was five. Sang like a pro. Always in trouble about something."

"Sounds like a couple of girls I know," says Mom.

"Who, us?" Agnes pretends that her feelings are hurt.

But the conversation is different now. We just talk and smile and laugh and drink tea. Mrs. DeLuca mentions Grace a few more times, and Auntie Flora talks about Joe, and then it's on to music—because, of course, Joe had a wonderful way with an accordion and apparently Grace could belt out Dolly Parton hits with the best of them—and the Battle of the Bands, and what fun it's going to be listening to us kids tomorrow night.

When Mrs. DeLuca gets up to leave, she hugs us all, one after the other. She hugs Auntie Flora the longest, though, and I see that Auntie Flora is hugging her, tightly, right back.

"Thank you for coming. And for the pie. So thoughtful," says Mom at the door.

Agnes and I are in the kitchen clearing up the mugs and plates, while Auntie Flora supervises from her chair at the table.

"No, Sylvia. Thank you. Thank you so much. I feel…" A pause.

"Auntie Flora has a bit of gift," Mom says.

"She does!" Mrs. DeLuca laughs. "Thank you. Good night. And we'll see you tomorrow at the music contest, right?"

When Mom comes back into the kitchen, the four of us look at each other like no one knows quite what to say yet. Agnes and I certainly don't. We just spent an hour at the kitchen table talking with a woman who lost her little girl in a car accident. That's definitely not something we do every day.

But Auntie Flora just stands up from the table and smiles.

"Now, wasn't that lovely? She needed to talk, poor thing." She turns to go to her room and then looks back and points at me. "Get that fiddle tuned, Ducky. I'll be waiting for you."

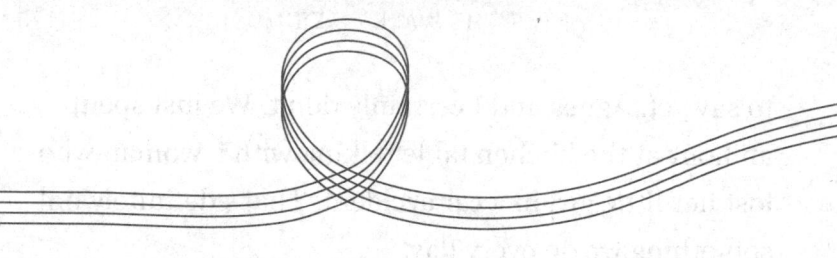

## Chapter 28

"FLORA!" AGNES YELLS UP THE STAIRS. "GET A MOVE ON! It's showtime!"

I take one more look at myself in the mirror. Yes, I look terrified. Because this is it. Battle of the Bands. My stomach gives a flip and I take a huge breath, smile at myself, and yell, "Coming!"

Mom, Agnes, and I have to sit together in the back seat for the drive over so that Auntie Flora can have the front seat beside Dad.

"I feel like a queen," she says and pretends to wave at some passing trees. Thank goodness there was no one on the sidewalk right then.

"I feel like a sardine," says Agnes.

Yes, it's a bit squishy back here. Especially since I insisted on keeping my violin with me.

"Really, Flora, just put it in the back." Agnes is probably regretting saying she'd come with us. Apparently Cedric, her new *boyfriend*, is going to meet us there and I bet she's thinking she should have just walked over with him.

"Nope. I need it with me."

"It's so big. It's like having a dog in the backseat with us."

"I'd love to have a dog." It's been on my wish list for years. (The things you think about when you're nervous, right?)

"Girls!" Mom's had enough.

"I had a dog named Bear," says Auntie Flora from the front seat. "Walked the children to school every day and came right home. And he looked like a bear, so no one ever gave him or the children any trouble."

More dog conversation follows, but I just hold my violin close like a favorite stuffy and think about the evening ahead. A warm-up with the quartet. Then down the hall for a warm-up with Crazy Train. I have no idea which band is performing when. And do we wait backstage? Or do we get to sit in the audience and listen to the other bands? Or maybe in the wings? And when they announce the winners, what happens then? And what would happen if Simon and I win? What would my friends—

"Here we are," says Dad.

And, now, here I am. In Practice Room 3 with my friends.

♪

"One more run-through, okay?" says Vlad. "Let's play it just once more."

"Vlad. Listen. It's not going to help us do anything better at this point," says Kristy.

"Come on. We all know we don't need help," says Bas. "Right?" He looks around at us and we all laugh.

"It's okay, Vlad. We're ready," I say, and I truly believe it.

I think we all believe it.

"Okay, okay. I guess we're good to go." Vlad gives in and shrugs.

It's just the four of us in Practice Room 3, where we've been assigned to warm up before the competition. We were told to be here early so the contest committee—that includes Mr. Herndorff—could be sure we're actually here. Oh, and give us some practice time, as well.

In a minute I'll go down the hall to the room where Simon and Keenan are waiting and we'll probably have this same conversation about whether or not to run through our piece one more time, although something tells me Keenan's too chill to want to do that.

I'm not feeling very chill at the moment.

"I have to go," I stand up and they all look at me.

"Now?" Kristy asks.

"I just want to check in with them," I say and head to the door.

But before I get there, Mr. Herndorff appears.

"Oh, Flora. Good, I was just about to tell you that you can go to the Crazy Train practice room now. Number 5. Just wait, though," he looks around at all of us. "Here's the order of performers tonight."

He consults a piece of paper in his hand and we exchange a look. *Not first, please not first.*

"Okay. First: Big Kids on the Playground."

We silently cheer but don't let him see, of course.

"Then: No Service, The Arden String Quartet, The Riverside Trio, and," he looks up at me, "last but not least, Crazy Train."

Okay, last is not terrible. It means Crazy Train can end the whole thing with a memorable bang, but it also means I have to play, then sit and listen to another group, and then play again. Maybe that gap will give me a chance to switch gears in my head, too?

"You get the closing spot," says Kristy, and I can't tell from her voice whether she's happy for me or not. I mean, it's not as if we're the main act closing the show or something. Right now, feeling more and more nervous, I'm not sure I want to know what she thinks, either.

Vlad raises his bow in classic questioning mode.

"Mr. Herndorff, do we wait here until our turn? Or do we get to hear the other bands?"

"It's easier if you listen from back here," he says. "Instruments and set up, et cetera. You can watch from the wings with your instruments, then you just have to walk on when it's your turn. I'll be there with Miss Cheng to help set up chairs. And you don't need music stands, right? So it should be very straightforward."

"Good thing Rudy and his band are going first," says Vlad. "Their set-up will take a few minutes."

"Can I go to the other practice room now?"

Yes, I interrupt this conversation because I'm feeling more and more nervous. Maybe it will help if I check in with Simon and Keenan.

"Good idea, Flora," says Mr. Herndorff. "I was just there, and, well, yes. Good idea. Go see how it's going."

Which is oddly cryptic, but I don't give it much thought as I go out the door and head down the hall to Practice Room 5.

Where I find Simon, alone.

# Chapter 29

SIMON LOOKS UP AS I WALK THROUGH THE DOOR, AND I can tell from the way his shoulders sag that I am not the person he was hoping to see.

"Oh, it's you," he says.

Nice.

"What?" My stomach gives a sudden jump. Something is wrong here. "Where's Keenan?"

"I don't know," he says and holds up his phone. "I've been texting him and he's not replying."

"Maybe he's on his way?"

"Yeah, maybe."

We stand there, frozen, and look at each other, thinking the same thing.

*What if Keenan doesn't show up?*

"I'll try him again," says Simon, eyes on his phone. "It's ringing, but..."

He lets it ring for ages then clicks it off. Checks texts. Nothing.

"So, what's happening here, guys?" Mr. Herndorff is at the door. "Still no word?"

Simon shakes his head.

"Okay, we're going to get started in about five minutes with the first group," says Mr. Herndorff. "Let's not panic. I'm going to ask Margaret to follow up and see if she can find out what's going on. You all gave a contact number on your registration and she has all the paperwork, so leave that with me."

He sounds calm. Like a teacher. He can probably see that I'm standing there frozen in place (in fear?) and Simon is practically vibrating with nerves, chewing his lip and staring at his phone.

"And maybe while the first two groups get going, you could talk about what you're going to do if Keenan doesn't show up, okay? Make a plan?" He smiles at us then. "Relax, kids. I know this isn't what you planned for. If you want to withdraw, of course that's perfectly understandable, but, hey..."

We both look at him, and he smiles at us.

"The show must go on, and all that. I believe in you."

He leaves, and we can hear him out in the hall calling Rudy and his big band— "Come on, Kids! The Playground's ready for you!" Lots of voices and people walking past the door. Somebody has a tambourine, I think, because it's jingling as they go past us towards the stage.

Simon goes over and shuts the door.

"What do you think?"

I'm still frozen in place, which is not good because very soon I'm going to have to go on stage and play that soaring violin line from "Lightning's Theme." Do I even remember how it goes? The decision the quartet made to memorize the piece and perform without music in front of us seems like a very bad one right now.

"I—I don't know what to think," I say.

"Do you want to just cancel?"

"Maybe he'll still get here. Can we wait a bit longer?" I don't want to be the one to make a call like that.

"No," says Simon. He takes a deep breath. "We need to make a decision. I say we…"

His phone buzzes.

"It's him," he says, reading the screen. "*Guys. Bad news. Fell off bike. Broken arm. At hospital. Sorry. Typing with one hand.*"

He looks up and I bet our faces have that same expression on them.

"He's not coming."

"He's not coming." I repeat. Maybe if I say it a few more times I'll be able to process what it means.

It's funny what happens to your brain when you get bad news. You go all cold, then hot. You stop thinking clearly. That is exactly what is happening to me as I stand there looking at Simon. I have a feeling the same thing is happening to him.

Okay. *Okay. Think, Flora.*

And the first thing that flashes through my mind is that Keenan isn't coming because he is sitting in a hospital with a broken arm.

Right. I know where to start.

"That's terrible," I say. "Text him back and tell him to feel better."

"What?"

"Tell him not to worry."

Simon hesitates, shakes his head, then texts back. Lets his hand drop, and we just stand there.

"Now what?" he says.

"Now, we make a plan."

"A plan. Okay. What plan?"

Something—an image—is taking shape in my head,

in my ears, under my fingers.

"Text your dad," I say.

"My dad?" Simon shakes his head at me as if I just said something completely strange. "My dad can't help us. He can't get up there on stage with us."

"No, he can't. But he can still help."

And I tell him my plan.

In the copy-reader's further shock,
Myra opened her eyes.
"Alvarado?" Johnson shouted in spite of myself. I just
said something completely at stake. "I'd died even I bit lip.
at. He said I got up there, making, with me.
No, he can't. But he was still help.
And I tell him tompton.

# Chapter 30

"THE ARDEN STRING QUARTET WILL NOW PERFORM 'LIGHTning's Theme' from the *Final Fantasy* soundtrack. The members of the quartet are first violin: Flora Parsons, second violin: Bas Malik, viola: Kristy Carpenter, cello: Vladimir Bachman."

We didn't know that Mrs. García was going to be the Mistress of Ceremonies, but here she is at the microphone as we walk on to applause and take our seats in our familiar quartet formation.

And something about that familiar, well-rehearsed formation really works for me right now because it's been a wild half-hour since Simon closed the door of Practice Room 5 and said to me, "What do you think?"

Rudy and his Big Kids on the Playground kicked things off with a fantastic garage band version of something from the indie rock catalog. Peering out at the audience from the wings, I could see all the parents (okay, my dad) loving it.

The judges loved it too.

"Turning a classic into something fresh," they said. "Such a creative arrangement, especially the trumpet. Such energy."

All true.

"Great job!" Vlad started the high-fives as they came off the stage.

"Where's Simon and Keenan?" Kristy whispered to me as we stood there watching The Riverside Trio take their positions for their performance of a Gordon Lightfoot classic. The judges loved it, too.

"Tight harmony. Guitar and piano accompaniment with unexpected ornamentation," they said.

"Um, practicing," I whispered to Kristy without looking at her. If she saw my face, she would have known that I was lying.

I hope Simon is exactly where he's supposed to be.

"Don't tell anyone," he said to me after texting his dad. "Just in case it doesn't work out."

Okay, so we have a little drama going on. And, of

course, that drama is in my head as I sit with my violin in "wait" position on my knee and watch for the signal from Vlad to lift it under my chin.

He looks at the three of us, gives a big nod of his head, and we lift our instruments into position. Still watching him, we follow his count, and then, we launch.

And the magic happens, as it always does. I'm completely swept away by the wave of sound our instruments send out over the audience. Why did I ever doubt them when they picked this piece? It's beautiful. It's magic.

I close my eyes for a few seconds and just play.

And when I open my eyes, I catch a glimpse of Mr. DeLuca easing carefully past a few people in the row of seats and sitting down beside Mrs. DeLuca. They exchange a look and a nod.

I hold a note a beat too long and get a slightly raised eyebrow from Vlad, but it doesn't matter, because we're on the last few bars and no one would notice. Just a bit of improvisation. Syncopation. I meant to do that.

The applause is huge, complete with a couple of *bravos*. Thanks, Agnes.

It's done. Kristy and Bas and I smile at each other in relief. Vlad is too busy smiling out at the audience and sending his vibes towards the panel of judges.

Yes, there's Dr. Ennis-Holt looking just as formal and cranky as I remember him.

But then he gives the judges' feedback.

"I have heard this ensemble perform before, and all I can say is, they get better and better. That was an accomplished performance, not just in the precision and musicianship of the playing, but also in the emotion that these young musicians brought to a piece with which I am unfamiliar. What this performance did was make us want to hear more. Very, very well done." And then, just as we're about to stand and leave, he adds: "Well coached, as well."

He gives a nod in our general direction, which I think is actually a nod for Mr. Herndorff. *Teaching, Lawrence?*

We're relieved and happy as we walk formally off the stage and then, once out of sight of the audience, collapse into a crazy group hug.

"Awesome!"

"You guys, we did so good!"

"Did you hear what he said?"

"I'm so glad we played that piece," I say to them all. It's a sort of apology, I guess, and I think they know that. "I loved every minute of that performance."

"So did I!" Mr. Herndorff is there too. "You were

perfection! You may not win this thing—you know, rock bands and the wow factor—but you should be very proud of yourselves." But before we can soak that in, he turns to me. "Um, Flora? You might want to get down to Practice Room 5."

Right. I'm not done yet.

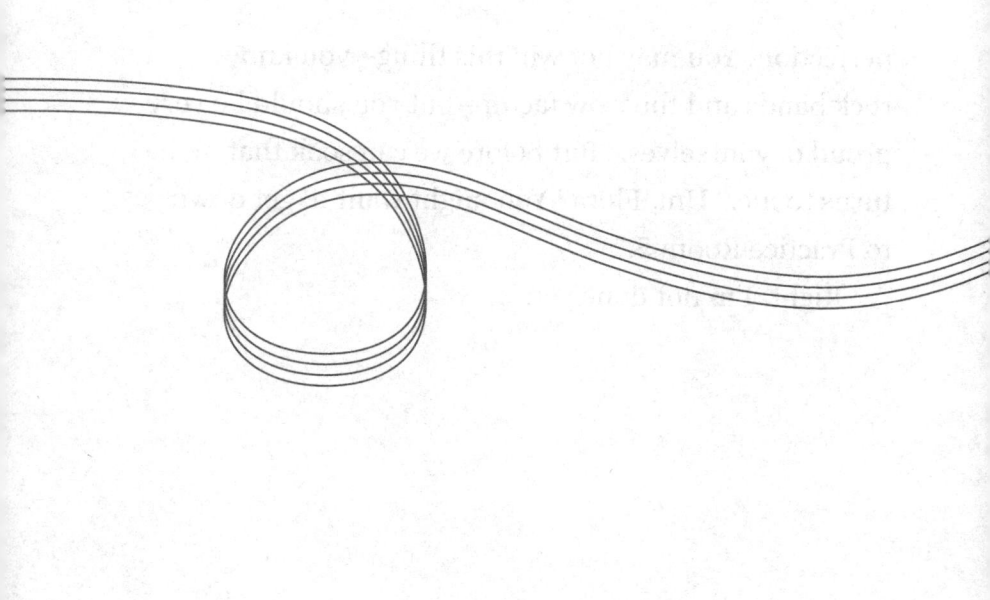

## ♪ Chapter 31

SIMON AND I WALK OUT ON STAGE, JUST THE TWO OF US.

Mr. Herndorff has set two chairs, slightly facing each other, and we sit.

Me with my fiddle, Simon with his bodhran.

Yes, the bodhran that he texted his dad to hurry home and bring back from the studio upstairs.

"There is a change in the program," Mrs. García says at the microphone. "Crazy Train is made up of three musicians, Keenan Dalvanian on keyboards and vocals, Flora Parsons on violin, and Simon DeLuca on bass guitar. Unfortunately, Keenan is unable to be here tonight, but Flora and Simon have decided to perform anyway. And may I say," Mrs. G.'s voice is suddenly much less formal, "kudos to these two young musicians for finding a way to share their music with us, despite the unexpected difficulties. They are going to—"

But she has to stop because the audience starts clapping.

I've been looking at Mrs. G., just trying to stay focused and ready...but really, this whole idea could go very badly, who knows? We haven't rehearsed or anything. What was I thinking? And why would Simon agree to it?

That's what's going through my head when the applause starts, and it surprises me so much that I glance at Simon.

He looks perfectly calm. He's even brushed his bangs to the side so I can see his face, his eyes, and he's looking out at the audience. Smiling.

I look out at the audience to see what he's smiling at. Of course, his parents. And, oh, so sweet, I can see them holding hands.

And right beside them I see Mom and Dad, and Agnes and Cedric. And Auntie Flora. She's not clapping, but she's looking right at me and nodding.

*Play me some tunes, Ducky.*

So that's exactly what we do.

# Chapter 32

WE DON'T WIN THE BATTLE OF THE BANDS.

Rudy and his garage band win, and he gives the best acceptance speech ever. He has everyone—participants, parents, teachers—laughing so hard we're crying.

He also thanks Simon.

"Hey man," he says, holding up the winning trophy and pointing down at Simon in the front row, where all the performers sit while the prize is announced. "When I gave up that percussion gig to you in music class, I knew I'd found my calling. My heart is with the trumpet now! Thanks for kicking me out of the percussion section, man."

The audience loves it. Simon points at him and they

do some weird in-the-air handshake or tribute to each other. The audience loves that too.

The end of the evening is noisy and wild, of course, with parents and students and everyone milling around, talking, getting instruments packed up. I see Mr. Herndorff talking to Dr. Ennis-Holt, who is nodding and listening intently. That's nice. Dad's talking to Simon's parents.

There's a reception in the foyer, but we don't stay long because Mom and Dad have organized something at home.

"An after-party," says Mom.

"A what?"

She winks. "Oh, just a few people. Back at the house."

"A few people" turns out to be Vlad, Bas, Kristy, Simon, and their parents, too. It's a full house, with people taking over the living room—Auntie Flora sits at the end of the couch and it's a revolving door of people coming to sit beside her and chat—and more people in and out of the kitchen, and through to the dining room, where there's snacks and sandwiches and pie (thanks to Mrs. DeLuca, who is a pie wizard, we have all learned).

"You guys were so good," Kristy says to me as we stand by the snacks eating way too many chips and sipping pop.

She means me and Simon.

"He really is a good musician," she says. "I guess it's not surprising."

We look over at Simon, Vlad, and Bas in the living room. I see Simon lift his hands as if he's holding an imaginary bodhran, while Vlad and Bas nod and ask questions.

"He is," I say. "He's also nice."

"You like him?" She gives me a look.

I shrug. "I don't know. But I don't hate him." I turn to her and say something that maybe I should have said a long time ago. "And he's not rude. He's not a snob. I think he's just sad sometimes, and a little shy."

Kristy bites her lip and nods. "I know. You're right. I'm sorry, about before, I don't know why I was acting so jealous."

I give her hand a squeeze and I know everything is going to be okay between us.

"Alright, everyone," Dad calls out so that people all over the house can hear. "Auntie Flora has requested a few tunes, so I would ask Flora and Simon and any other interested musicians to please get your gear and let's set up in the living room here."

And that's what happens.

I lead the tunes, and Kristy and Bas follow along as

best they can on viola and violin. Sometimes they just play a drone accompaniment, and that's fine, too.

Simon plays the bodhran, and since the rule is that you can only have one drum at a session, no one else tries to thump on anything.

Auntie Flora asks Dad to demonstrate the spoons for Vlad, and before long, Vlad has become an expert.

I run through the easy dance tunes like "Mussels in the Corner" and "She Said She Couldn't Dance" and "Coming From the Races" and everyone claps along.

Then it's on to some of the trickier ones, and that's just Simon and me, with everyone clapping along and laughing when the extra beats throw them off.

Auntie Flora laughs and claps, too, and calls out tune suggestions sometimes. She sings along when there are lyrics.

"We are having a time," she says to me when I take a break and squeeze in beside her. "But there's one thing I'd love you to play. Maybe you and Agnes?"

I know what she wants to hear, and she doesn't even have to say it.

## 𝄞 Chapter 33

BAS'S PARENTS ARE SAYING THEIR GOODBYES NOW, MOVing towards the door. And I can see the Bachmans are looking at their watches.

Yes, the party is nearly over.

"Before everyone goes," I say, with an arm around Auntie Flora. "There's one more song we need to do. It's my Auntie Flora's favorite, and it's easy to sing along to. So maybe we can end with it?"

And that's what happens. People shift around so that Agnes is sitting next to Auntie Flora on the couch, and I sit on the footstool, on her other side. I play the first few notes and the three of us start to sing,

*"Her smile was shy the day we met..."*

Soon the whole room is singing along. Everyone picks up on the chorus, and I even hear some harmony. My fiddle is the only instrument this time. My fiddle, and all our voices, singing this sad song that, for some reason doesn't feel as sad to me tonight.

Instead, it feels warm. Like family. Like a hug. Everyone sings until I finish with a few last notes, and then there's a huge wash of applause and the evening is over.

The DeLucas don't leave right away, and I'm happy about that, because Simon and I have hardly had a chance to talk about our performance. It was so busy at the competition, and then the reception, and this after party here, where he spent most of his time with the boys.

So when Agnes and Cedric decide they're going to go for a late-night walk; and Auntie Flora, Mom, and Mrs. Deluca go to the kitchen for one more cup of tea (or maybe wine?); and the dads go down to the basement to check out Dad's vinyl collection in the rec room; Simon and I find ourselves in the living room, still holding our instruments and completely exhausted.

Well, I am, anyway.

I lean back on the couch and give a huge sigh.

"Wow."

He's still holding his bodhran as he sits beside me and leans back.

"Yeah. Wow."

"It was good," I say. "Tonight."

He doesn't say anything for a moment, but he's smiling. Eyes closed. Relaxed. He nods.

"It was good," he says. "Thank you."

"For what?"

"For your good idea. For not freaking out when we found out Keenan couldn't make it. For playing so well."

"You played great, too. We wowed them."

"Crazy Train did not go off the rails. Should've won."

"Totally should've won."

We both laugh.

Our mothers are laughing, too. Auntie Flora says something and they all laugh again.

"I haven't seen my mom this happy since—in a long time," he says. "Did you see her singing along to that song you guys did with your aunt?"

I look over at him. His eyes are open now and he's looking—somewhere. Up. I'm pretty sure he's not looking at our living room ceiling.

"Nice song," he says. "I should learn that one. What's it called?"

"Time is a Fickle Friend."

*Is now the right time? Is there ever a right time for this kind of conversation?*

I take a deep breath.

*I hope you're right, Auntie Flora.*

"Tell me about her," I say.

He turns to look at me. "Who?"

"Tell me about your little sister," I say. "Tell me about Grace."

# The End 𝄢

# Time is a Fickle Friend

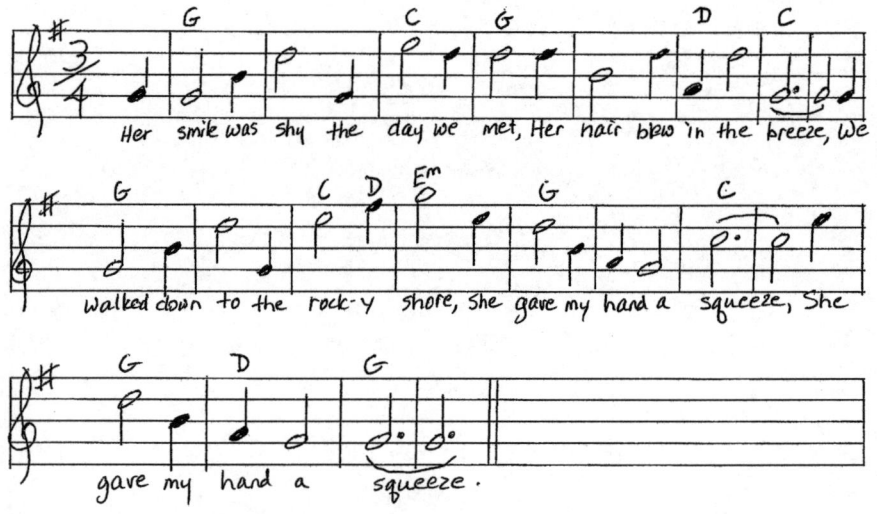

# Lyrics

♪

Her smile was shy the day we met,
Her hair blew in the breeze,
We walked down to the rocky shore,
She gave my hand a squeeze,
She gave my hand a squeeze.
Our hearts were joined from that day on,
Our time would know no end,
But clouds do come, and waves do roll,
And time's a fickle friend,
And time's a fickle friend.
Today I stood out on the shore
The day was bright and fine,
I felt her near, I heard her voice
And felt her hand in mine,
And felt her hand in mine.
The clouds may come, the waves may roll,
And time keeps us apart,
But always will my Brigus girl
Be smiling in my heart,
Be smiling in my heart.

# After the Wallpaper Music

♪

# A Playlist

Flora and her friends encounter a wide variety of music in *After the Wallpaper Music*. In fact, there are a number of real compositions mentioned in this story—readers may already be familiar with some of them. If not, this list gives you an opportunity to explore and listen to the music that is so important to Flora and her musical friends and family.

## Classical/Orchestral

♪ *String Quartet, Op 76 No 3, "Emperor"*
(COMPOSER: JOSEPH HAYDN)

♪ *Final Fantasy XIII "Lightning's Theme"*
(COMPOSER: MASASHI HAMAUZU)

## Rock

♪ *Don't Stop Believin'* (JOURNEY)
♪ *Crazy Train* (OZZY OSBOURNE)
♪ *Livin' on a Prayer* (BON JOVI)
♪ *Solsbury Hill* (PETER GABRIEL)

## Traditional

♪ *Cumberland Gap*
(AMERICAN FOLK SONG AND FIDDLE TUNE)

♪ *Soldier's Joy*
(SCOTTISH/AMERICAN FIDDLE TUNE)

♪ *Father's Jig*
(IRISH/NEWFOUNDLAND FIDDLE TUNE)

♪ *Kitty's Rambles*
(IRISH/NEWFOUNDLAND FIDDLE TUNE)

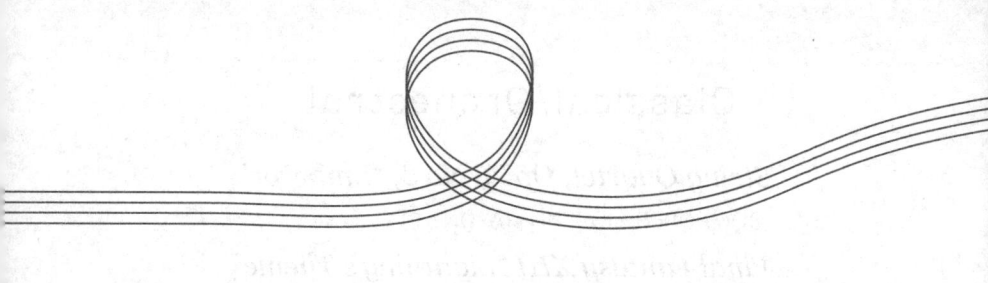

# Acknowledgments

Writing this story of a girl and her musical adventures was such fun for me—because I'm a lot like Flora, experimenting with different styles of music, learning different instruments, and sharing music with friends in tune sessions, song circles, and even on stage at festivals and concerts. I drew on my own experience for much of the story, but I did have some help, too.

Years ago I met Newfoundland traditional musicians Jean Hewson and Christina Smith at a music camp. I knew a lot about traditional music already, but over the years of our friendship, they've taken me deep into the music of their province, for which I am forever grateful. Auntie Flora, with her love of tunes and songs, is a character based on that unique musical spirit Jean and Christina shared with me. Thanks, Duckies!

A pivotal scene needed just the right details. So, thank you to musician and music educator Sandy Wright for his suggestion of scales that work for warming up band and string instruments together.

I'm grateful to the Ontario Arts Council for providing financial assistance during the writing of this book.

The team at Pajama Press embraced this story and made the entire editorial process incredibly easy for me. Thank you, Emma, Quinn, Simin, and Gail, for welcoming Flora and me so enthusiastically.

And, as ever, love and gratitude to my family for always cheering me on.

# Interview with Jean Mills

♪ **What inspired you to write this story?**

This story began with my love of traditional Newfoundland music—the songs and tunes I've learned, listened to, and performed. It's such a distinct repertoire and I wanted to share it with readers who may not have encountered it before. Also, I've always found joy and comfort in music. Showing how music can pull people together—especially people who may be in need of joy and comfort—was definitely a spark for the story.

♪ **Are you also a musician? If so, what instruments can you play?**

I am a musician, yes! I started out as a musical kid playing recorder in school and launched myself from there. My musical adventures include lots of singing, as well as recorder, whistle, piano, ukulele, guitar, viola, and—my favorite—Appalachian dulcimer. Since childhood, I've been studying, composing, and performing music at concerts, events, schools, and folk festivals. I've been in a few bands and even recorded some music. But I'm not a natural performer as I get very nervous, so now I just love playing at local traditional music sessions, singing along with family and friends around the firepit, and playing for my own enjoyment. Traditional folksong is of special interest. As I wrote Flora's story, I wanted to include a familiar Irish/Newfoundland song called "Sweet Forget-Me-Not," but then I decided it might be more fun to write something original, so I did! That song is "Time Is A Fickle Friend."

♪ How does song writing differ from writing prose?

I think writing lyrics to a song is like writing poetry—it's just another form of storytelling. You still have to find a voice and tell a story. But, of course, then you have to make sure the words fit the rhythm and patterns of the melody, and that can take a lot of revision. Sometimes the words come first, which is what happened with "Time Is A Fickle Friend." But sometimes it's the melody that drives the creative process, and the lyrics have to be carefully crafted. It's a challenging creative process involving two of my favorite things—words and music—and I love it.

♪ How long did it take you to write this story? What's your writing process?

This story took over a year to write, but that's normal for me because I have an unusual writing process. I always have more than one project in progress, so my focus may be somewhere else for weeks or months at a time. I'm not a "write every day" kind of writer, which is a bit unusual, I think. I believe that most of the work happens before even putting words on paper, so I spend a lot of time thinking, hearing the characters' voices, and imagining scenes and conversations. I write one draft, revising as I go. When I have a finished draft, it's very close to its final form and doesn't need a full rewrite. It might take longer, but it's a process that works for me.

♪ Have you envisioned what happens after the events in the book?

First, I see Flora and her friends being inspired by all the new music they encountered through the Battle of the Bands competition and branching out to try new musical genres together. I also think Flora and Simon will become close friends, maybe even becoming a couple as they move into their teens. They have forged a strong connection throughout this story, and I think there's more in store for them.

♪ Did you have any alternative endings in previous drafts?

No, this story was always going to be about Flora finding a way to connect with Simon through music, and that's exactly where the story ends. I did consider having Crazy Train win the Battle of the Bands with their alternate performance, but I decided that wasn't necessary—and it might be a bit too predictable!

♪ What scene in the book are you most proud of, and why?

I spent a long time on the scene in the Parsons' kitchen, when Auntie Flora encourages Petra to talk about Grace. It was important to make it an emotional moment, but not too sentimental or dramatic. I feel that scene tells us a lot about Auntie Flora's strength, as well as her approach to life and loss, while also imparting lessons that are crucial to Flora's interactions with Simon. I had to get the tone right, and it took some work.

♪ Who is your favorite character in the book?

I love Simon. He's flawed and definitely hurting, but he's kind and caring, too. I worked hard to make sure Flora sees that side of him when others just see him being "rude" or distant. And, of course, Auntie Flora is the elderly relative we all need in our lives!